STAR LIGHT,
STAR BRIGHT

Other books by Sydell Voeller:

Unlikely Dad
Daisies Are Forever

STAR LIGHT, STAR BRIGHT

•

Sydell Voeller

AVALON BOOKS
NEW YORK

Published by Thomas Bouregy & Co., Inc.
160 Madison Avenue, New York, NY 10016

Library of Congress Cataloging-in-Publication Data

Voeller, Sydell.
Star light, star bright / Sydell Voeller.
p. cm.
ISBN-13: 978-0-8034-9815-0 (acid-free paper)
ISBN-10: 0-8034-9815-2 (acid-free paper) 1. Single mothers—
Fiction. 2. Oregon—Fiction. I. Title.

PS3572.O275S73 2007
813'.6—dc22
2006028589

PRINTED IN THE UNITED STATES OF AMERICA
ON ACID-FREE PAPER
BY HADDON CRAFTSMEN, BLOOMSBURG, PENNSYLVANIA

198ρ

54026

Chapter One

"Oh no!" Chyenna Dupres felt a hot wave of embarrassment, contrasting the chill of the nocturnal desert air.

Here she was, in nearly nothing but her birthday suit, and she just realized she was in someone else's van! One glance at the Stetson she'd almost sat on told her she'd blown it big time.

Feeling like a blundering idiot, she yanked on her thermal underwear. This van, one of a few hundred vehicles parked alongside the dusty road, had looked so much like her own in the darkness. Still, *anyone* could've done this, she tried to console herself. She'd read in the daily paper, the *Oregonian,* that Indianhead Springs, the site for the amateur astronomy campout, was chosen for its exceptional dark skies.

1

"Mama! Where are you?" The sound of her nine-year-old daughter's voice snapped her from her thoughts. She peered through the half-opened van door. There was Mandy, barely visible, back turned, standing a short distance away.

"Mandy! Over here!" Chyenna called in a stage whisper.

The girl spun around. "Mama?"

"Yes! I'll be right there!"

A pause followed, then a shrill, "What are you doing—"

"Shh! I'll explain in a minute."

"Hurry! I can't find the porta-potties! I gotta go!"

Chyenna finished dressing, then scrambled outside and led the way. They passed a string of tents, campers, and trailers where most of the others were camped, their telescopes and cars close by. Small groups were clustered, speaking in technical jargon Chyenna didn't understand—and didn't care to. Spending this special time with Mandy camping under the stars was all she needed right now.

Half serious, half laughing, she told Mandy about the details of her humiliating mishap. They giggled so hard they had to stop walking to splint their aching sides. It felt so good . . . good to be finally laughing.

A short time later they returned to their campsite. Chyenna had pitched their tent several hundred yards from the road beneath the towering pine trees where a few other shade-loving souls had also camped. Though the forested canopy protected them from the scorching desert sun, it also meant a longer trek back to the van to get food or gear. Forest Service regulations required all vehicles to be parked near the road to allow a quick exit in case of fire.

"It's awesome here!" Mandy exclaimed as they carted two reclining lawn chairs onto a grassy clearing, then sat down.

"Yes, gorgeous!" Chyenna tipped her head back for a long moment and sighed. Masses of stars winked against a canopy of midnight blue. Never, *ever* had she seen the Milky Way with such brilliance, such clarity. She beamed her flashlight onto the star chart she held on her lap, then peered up again. "Look! The Northern Cross."

"Where?"

"Right there." She pointed. "Straight overhead!"

"Oh, wow! *Now* I see it! That's cool!"

They continued star hopping from one constellation to another. Chyenna recounted aloud the age-old myths about each, while Mandy listened, fascinated.

"Where'd you learn those stories, Mama?"

"In college. Greek literature, I think."

"Pardon me, ma'am." A voice. A definitely male voice.

She looked up, surprised. She hadn't even heard anyone approaching.

"Do you mind shutting off that damned flashlight?" he said, his words edged with irritation.

"What?"

"You heard me. Your flashlight. Turn it off!"

The man towered over her. Broad shoulders and a lanky frame were concealed inside a heavy jacket and tight-fitting jeans. Though it was too dark to discern his facial features, she caught the faint scent of aftershave, which mingled with the dusty smells of the desert.

She flipped off the light, then stood up, straightening to her full five and a half feet. "Happy?" she asked.

"Obviously you didn't read the rules in the registration packet," he went on, ignoring her impudent retort. He took a step closer. She could see a bit more of his chiseled profile, the stubborn set of his jaw. A shiver of awareness rippled down her spine. He appeared so male, so ruggedly powerful.

"No, as a matter of fact, I didn't," she shot back. "Mandy and I've been busy." Truth was, they'd spent the last two frustrating hours trying to drive their tent stakes into the rocky desert floor. Yet this was apparently a guy who played by the rules—whatever they were—and it was plain he wasn't going to let her off easy. "What rule could we be possibly breaking?"

"Our red light policy. No white light allowed after dark. Red only." Crossing his arms over his chest, he rocked back on his heels. "White light interferes with night vision more than you obviously realize, and *your* white light, lady, is no exception."

"Oh, give me a break. Surely this one little flashlight can't make that much difference." She refused to allow this man to humiliate her so, especially in front of

Mandy, though right now her daughter appeared more intent on rummaging through the cooler than listening to their verbal sparring.

"Trust me, it *does* make a difference," the man continued. "I've got a line of folks waiting to take a look through my telescope, and if they can't see as good as they should, I'm gonna lose big bucks."

"Oh, I get it. You must be one of those hot-shot astrophotographers," she retorted. "Who else would be so uptight about a little white light?"

"No, I'm just your average amateur astronomer— that is, when I'm not minding the ranch. We raise cattle, Herefords. On the side, I make custom telescopes and sell them."

She bit her lip, considering. Now that was an interesting combination, though certainly not an impossibility. Goodness only knew, this valley was marked by memories of frontier days when cowboys roamed the unsettled plains. Then too, the annual rodeo and county fair every Labor Day weekend was still the biggest event of the summer.

"This your daughter?" he asked, his voice softening a little. By now Mandy was stretched out again on the lawn chair, ankles crossed, chomping a granola bar.

"Yes. Her name's Amanda. I'm Chyenna." She didn't bother to give their last name, nor any explanations why they were camping alone.

"Howdy," he said, extending his large gloveless hand. His grip was strong, enveloping, and hot, despite the night air. "I'm Blair Westerman. I've a daughter about Amanda's age—maybe a little older. Name's Lisa."

"Wow! Someone to hang out with!" Mandy exclaimed. "Where is she?"

"Sleeping in our tent."

"Oh. Can I meet her tomorrow then?"

"Reckon so. Anyway, you're bound to run into her sooner or later."

About my astronomically incorrect red flashlight," Chyenna interrupted before they could get too chummy. "Got any ideas about how I can make it right?"

"Sure. A few strips of taillight repair tape, and you got it. Matter of fact, I just happen to have a new package back at my campsite. If you'd like to head over there with me, I'll give you some."

She stiffened. "No thanks. I'll think of some other way of improvising. And for now, Mandy and I won't need our star charts anyway," she was quick to add. "We can always make up our own constellations."

He gave a brusque laugh. "Now that's what I like. A self-sufficient woman." She thought she detected a flash of amusement in his eyes before he turned and sauntered back into the blackness.

Blair Westerman sat outside his tent, watching the night turn to dawn. The first rays of sunlight were showing, transforming the skies from a dusky cobalt blue to washes of mauve-orange. All was quiet now, amazingly quiet, except for the sound of his little daughter's gentle, even breathing from inside the tent.

Man, what a night! The skies had been dark and clear as glass, a perfect ten. And the moons of Jupiter had been outstanding. Why, it had been tempting to go get that plucky little lady he'd talked to—her girl too— and invite them to take a look through his telescope— anything to spend just a few more minutes with her. Let's see, what did she say their names were? Chyenna and Amanda? Yep, that was it . . .

But she probably would've refused his invitation flat out, he reminded himself. After all, she hadn't taken too kindly to him informing her about the white light rule, and now that he thought back on it, maybe he *had* come on to her a little too strong. Besides, he couldn't help sensing that all she'd wanted was to be left alone.

Yes, even when they'd first arrived during twilight, he'd seen the haunted look on her face, sensed her quiet desperation. In the beginning, he'd been intrigued, even attracted to her. He'd found it hard to resist the sight of her long mane of hair, the color of molasses, the way it swung gently with her every graceful move. And what a figure in those snug designer jeans! Enough to put a rodeo queen to shame.

But soon the attraction had evolved into something more . . . concern, maybe. A desire to help. Try as he did, he couldn't brush aside the nagging thought she might be running from something.

Or someone.

But why? Who?

At first it appeared as if they were going to sleep in their van, but then she'd finally hauled out that pitiful excuse for a two-man tent. The entire time she'd struggled to drive in the stakes, he'd held back offering his help. If she was as proud as Martha—and from the looks of it, she probably was—she'd turn him down anyway.

Martha. Unbidden, his thoughts turned back to the four years they'd lived in L.A.—the drive-by shooting . . . the look of regret in the emergency room doctor's eyes when he'd said there was no hope of saving her.

He heaved a sigh, then stared unseeingly at a distant hill. One year ago. Somehow, it seemed like forever. He and Martha had been happily married, as happy as any two people could be. Well, almost, that is. Martha had always been a big-city girl. They'd met their senior year in college at Eastern Oregon State, had fallen promptly in love, and soon after graduation, they'd married. Though she'd tried her best to make a new life for herself in Prairie Valley, she'd grown more depressed with each passing year. She yearned for the concrete and high-rises, the noise and the energy that pulsed through the crowded streets, she'd said. And here in the country, she'd felt as if she were dying a slow, agonizing death.

"College lasted only a few years, not a lifetime," was her quick reply every time he'd reminded her that the university where she'd studied also happened to be in a small town.

And so against his better judgment—for they had Lisa's future to consider as well—he gave in. He gave in and took Martha back to L.A. where she landed herself a position in a big advertising firm; he, a job with a major science catalogue distributor; and for Lisa a highly recommended nanny. Life would be perfect now, he'd promised Martha, though deep in his gut, he couldn't see how.

Then came the shooting, and that very bliss he'd promised her had so swiftly come to an end. If only he'd insisted they stay on the ranch, this tragedy would've never happened, he told himself over and over again. Afterward, he hadn't wasted a minute high-tailing it out of there, out of that noisy, dirty city, back to the simple country life he'd known for nearly three decades. Still, his guilt had only grown, haunting him, stalking him, nearly driving him clean out of his mind.

He massaged the back of his neck, then closed his eyes and yawned. Hell, he'd better get some sleep. Already Lisa was stirring and before long, she'd be pestering him to take her for another hike in the canyon, or worse, back into town for more junk food. Yep, junk food. That's what kids like best, don't they? Candy, soda, and potato chips, that sort of thing. He had to admit, he sometimes didn't have a clue when it came to raising his little daughter. But now, God bless her, Ma had stepped in and taken over. Her house was right be-

hind his on the hundred-and-fifty-thousand-acre spread
that made up the Lazy Y Ranch, a family operation that
he and his two brothers had taken over since their father
died of cancer ten years earlier.

He sighed again. At least there'd been another female who was willing to play the role of surrogate
mother. But even Ma had had a tough time filling
Martha's shoes. Despite her unhappiness, Martha had
been a very good mother . . .

*Don't think about Martha. Don't dwell on the memo-
ries. Memories can run a man right into the ground—
and you're already about to hit rock-bottom.*

"Ladies and gentleman, may I have your attention,
please?" the man's voice rang out.

It was late afternoon the following day, and the sun
scorched down in shimmering waves on Indianhead
Springs, where each rolling brown hill stretched to
meet the horizon. The earthy smells of sage, freckled
milkvetch, mixed with pine carried on a faint breeze.
Some nine hundred campers were gathered near the
registration tent, some sitting on camp stools and lawn
chairs, others standing. The Saturday program was
about to begin.

Chyenna fanned herself with a brochure as she listened to the man standing behind a makeshift podium,
a black metal music stand.

"My name is Blair Westerman, this year's president
of the Northwest Astronomers Association," he was

saying. "On behalf of all the club officers, I'd like to thank you for making this the best attended Star Party in our twelve-year history here in central Oregon."

So the man who'd humiliated her last night had a major role in organizing this event, she mused with growing interest. The club president, in fact.

As Blair Westerman smiled at the crowd, exposing a flash of even white teeth, she struggled to repress a fresh wave of awareness. Now that she could see him in the full light of day, he was even more ruggedly handsome than she'd dreamed. He wore tight denim jeans that molded trim hips and sculpted thighs. His white T-shirt strained against his well-muscled chest. Unlike the night before, when he'd worn a snugly fitting knit cap, he was now sporting a Stetson, which partially shadowed his alluring face.

Wait a minute! She narrowed her gaze as the realization slashed through her like a jagged knife. Could that be the same Stetson she almost sat on last night? Could the van she'd mistaken for her own belong to Blair Westerman?

Don't be ridiculous! her more reasonable self argued. *There are plenty others here with Stetsons just like that.* Besides, this Blair Westerman she'd talked with had said he was a cattle rancher. Surely he'd be driving a pickup instead, wouldn't he? Didn't all ranchers drive pickups?

"Before I introduce our guest speaker," he continued, flashing the crowd another lazy grin, "I have one an-

nouncement to make. Will the owner of the cell phone
and lipstick left in my van last night please contact me
as soon as possible? Though I don't have a clue how
they got there—not to mention the fact I already have
my own cell phone, and claim no earthly use for "Blaz-
ing Fuchsia" war paint—I *would* like to get them back
to their rightful owner."

Chyenna closed her eyes as a roar of laughter rose up
all around her. *Lord help me,* she prayed, feeling the
heat of embarrassment creep up in her cheeks.

She needed that phone. There was no way she could
avoid claiming it. She'd promised her business partner
at the inn, Nan Woodall, she'd keep it within earshot in
the event Nan needed to reach her. This was Nan's first
weekend to manage the place alone, and goodness only
knew, things hadn't been running too smoothly lately.
Why, only last week an unnamed citizen wrote an editorial for the town paper criticizing Chyenna's efforts to
attract tourism. Several of the locals had even stormed
inside the inn to voice their objections in person.

"Mama?" Mandy piped up. The girl tugged on
Chyenna's T-shirt. "Is that man up there talking about
you?"

Amused glances flashed their way. More laugher rippled through the crowd.

Gritting her teeth, Chyenna shot Mandy a warning
look. "Shh, darling. We'll deal with that later. Right
now the speaker's about to begin."

But listening to the speaker was the last thing

Chyenna did as the next hour passed by. All talk about the ever growing problem of global light pollution and recent discoveries made by the Hubble telescope barely penetrated her thoughts.

The memories of what should've been this thirteenth day of August were still too raw, too painful. Chyenna had been desperate for a distraction, *any* distraction, and hence her spur-of-the-moment decision to come here. She'd hoped against all hope that maybe on this desert mountaintop, she could at last find peace.

So far, she'd experienced everything but that— especially after she'd encountered Blair Westerman. Last night when she'd crawled into her sleeping bag and was drifting off to sleep, she'd vowed she would forget about him. And right now it was tempting to send Mandy to get the cell phone instead of facing him herself.

Shame on you! Shame on you for even entertaining that notion . . .

Inhaling a shaky breath, she glanced his way. No, she wasn't a coward. She'd face him. Own up to it like she should. But could she withstand still another onslaught of his rugged male magnetism?

Like it or not, she'd soon find out.

Chapter Two

"Excuse me, Mr. Westerman?" For the past several minutes, Blair had been chatting with a middle-aged couple who had just filled out an order form for one of his custom-made telescopes, a twelve-and-a-half-inch reflector, she'd heard them say. Mandy had wandered off to a planetarium show sponsored by the Junior Astronomer's Club, and Chyenna decided it was now or never. If she didn't approach him this very instant, she would undoubtedly lose her nerve.

He appeared not to have heard her.

"Excuse me," she repeated. "May I have a word with you, Mr. Westerman?"

He turned around. His eyes crinkled in an amused squint. "Oh! You again . . . Chyenna, didn't you say your name is?"

"Yes. Chyenna Dupres. I'm the one with the nine-year-old daughter," she added unnecessarily. She tried to decide by the tone of his voice whether he was surprised or irritated, but couldn't.

"Ah, yes." One corner of his mouth turned up in a hint of a smile. "So we meet again."

"We need to talk," she blurted. "As soon as you're free, that is."

"I'm free right now." He regarded her for a long moment, his eyebrows knitted together. "So what is it? How can I help you?"

"I'm the owner of the cell phone. I've come to claim it." She kept her eyes fixed squarely on his. For a dizzying instant, she felt breathless. She felt as if she could drown in those deep cerulean pools, as open and translucent as the cloudless desert sky above. It wasn't fair, she thought. It wasn't fair he should be such a heart-stopper. It wasn't fair he should wield such power.

She jerked her gaze away, staring off instead at an indefinite spot somewhere behind him.

"Well, talk about a coincidence," he drawled. "If it isn't the white light lady herself."

"Please, Mr. Westerman. I need my phone back," she said again, disregarding his apparent attempt to divert her, or worse, cause her to squirm. Whatever, he was making her sound like some disembodied spirit—an angel, perhaps—although after their heated discussion the night before, she doubted he'd consider her anything close to an angel.

His smile grew wider. "Let's forget the formalities. Just call me Blair."

"Fine then. Whatever . . ." Her face burned, and she knew it wasn't entirely because of the dry desert heat. Off to the side, she caught sight of a few other campers who wandered by, casting them curious looks.

"And I suppose it goes without saying the lipstick belongs to you too."

"Yes. Of course."

"What proof do I have they're really yours?" he asked. Especially the cell phone?"

She tipped her chin. "I'll describe it to you down to the last detail."

She did just that, apparently to his satisfaction, because before she could finished, he interrupted her.

"Okay, I'm convinced!" He spread his hands in a dismissive gesture. "But just one more small detail," he added. Subtle traces of amusement threaded his voice. "What were you doing in my van last night?"

"It's a long story . . . and one I don't feel like going into right now."

"Technically speaking, you had no business being there," he said. "In other words, I've every right to demand an explanation."

"All right. You've made your point." Her gaze swept the people who were milling about. Some were swapping eye pieces and lens filters, others comparing notes about the previous night's observing. "Uh . . . but first, could we go somewhere a little more private?"

He shrugged. "Might as well head back to my campsite. Your phone's locked inside my van."

"Where's your daughter?" she asked as she fell into step alongside of him. She was stalling, she couldn't deny it. How in the world was she going to explain she was using his van for a dressing room? It was simply too embarrassing. She was supposed to be a savvy business woman, for heaven's sake, not some idiotic bimbo who couldn't distinguish her own vehicle from someone else's.

"Lisa decided to go to the planetarium with the other kids. At first I was gonna leave her home with my mother this weekend—all this scientific stuff bores her so—but Ma talked me out of it. She keeps insisting I need to spend more time with Lisa, and maybe she's right. It's just—" He broke off, squaring his jaw, though he never for even a split second turned to glance at her.

"Just *what*?" she prompted.

"Nothing. Not important." Silence stretched between them as they passed by the fast food vendors, then the string of assorted tents and RVs.

"Mandy went to the kids' display too," she said at last, breaking the awkward silence. "I think it's great that the club sponsors special programs."

He shrugged again. "Yep, I reckon so. The Junior Astronomers' club is totally out of my league though. Two of our members who used to be teachers designed the planetarium. It's completely mobile, can be put up and

down like a gigantic umbrella. They travel from school
to school putting on programs, and I understand the
kids really go for it. So far, that's the only thing my
daughter has been interested in here."

"Oh. I bet Mandy and I can improve on that. Why
don't you send your daughter over to our camp tonight
while we make up our next episode of star myths and leg-
ends? Mandy loves storytelling. Maybe Lisa will too."

"You sure you can put up with another kid hanging
around?"

"Of course! The more the merrier, as the old saying
goes. Besides, you heard how excited Mandy was last
night after you mentioned you have a daughter too."

"Oh yeah. I'll pass on your invite to Lisa, then let her
decide." He smirked. "I'm sure she'll think anything is
better than sticking with her dull old dad."

"You don't give yourself enough credit."

"Believe me. I know what I'm talking about. Keeping Lisa busy was Martha's job."

Martha? His wife? Chyenna couldn't help noting
how he referred to her in the past tense. *Why? Had she
died? Had they divorced?*

"Where're you from?" he asked. He darted her a
sidelong glance.

"Prairie Valley—though I'm originally from Portland."

"Ah, a big city gal." A shadow swept across his face.
"As for me, I was born and raised here. The ranch has

been in my family for three generations. My grandfather homesteaded it in the 1920s."

"Long time, Mr. Westerman."

"Yes, it is. My kin believes in hard work and tradition. And I'm proud to be one of them."

As they ambled on, her shoulder brushed his side. Her heart raced like a trip hammer. Darn! This wasn't supposed to be happening! Why did this man get to her so? She didn't want it. She didn't want to be here with him like this, battling the swirling eddy of emotions that raged inside her. She had a job to do, and she refused to become sidetracked.

Ever since she'd first moved to Prairie Valley four months earlier, she'd promised herself two things. First, to turn her business into an unequivocal success. Second, to carve out a brand-new life for her daughter and herself—and to never, *ever* have to look back.

Yes, one full decade ago today, Chyenna mused. Ten years ago she'd stood before the altar with Daniel, pledging a love that was suppose to last a lifetime. Soon afterward, Daniel was promoted to vice president of the large insurance firm where he'd been working and they'd purchased their first home on the west hills of Portland. A year later Mandy was born. But while Chyenna was precariously balancing motherhood with her career as a commercial artist, Dan was attempting to balance *his* professional life with something else entirely.

A newfound lover.

On the heels of his betrayal had come the divorce, and now one full year had passed. A year that seemed more like a millennium, Chyenna had often thought. Yet on that fateful day, that day she held the divorce papers in her trembling hands, she'd silently pledged that from that moment on—no matter what the price—she would guard her heart forever.

Soon they arrived at Blair's campsite.

"Have a seat," he said, nodding toward a camp stool. "I'll get your phone and be right back."

His van was parked a short distance away. Her own vehicle was two cars down from his, which only served to remind her again of last night's fiasco. At the thought, a new humiliation washed over her.

"Thanks, but I really can't stick around," she told him. "I promised Mandy I'd meet her back at the planetarium when the program is over."

"Before you go, can I interest you in something cold to drink?" he asked, glancing back over his shoulder.

"Well—" She hesitated, "all right." What would it hurt, spending just a little more time with Blair Westerman, she reassured herself. The planetarium show wasn't due to end for another half hour or so, and right now a cold drink really did sound inviting.

"So what'll it be? I've got beer and Coke, and plenty of both."

"A Coke would be fine."

"One Coke coming right up!"

She sat down, then glanced around his campsite. On a compact folding table were scattered several star atlases, two books by Stephen Hawking, and another entitled *The Messier Album.* Blair's tent was dome-shaped, forest green, over twice the size of hers, and covered with a large plastic tarp. A giant-sized blue cooler, two more folded tarps, and a first aid kit were stacked neatly near the tent opening. Obviously he'd come better prepared than she had.

"I'm sorry," he said as he ambled back, grinning sheepishly. He held out the tube of lipstick. "It looks as if Lisa's been experimenting. I guess she *has* been bored. It's worn down practically to a nubbin."

She laughed in spite of herself. "No harm. Let her keep it. All I really care about is my phone."

"Well *that*, I'm pretty sure, hasn't been tampered with. I locked it up inside the glove compartment the minute I discovered it." He handed her the phone, a can of Coke, and sat down next to her. He was close, too close. But what was it that frightened her the most? Blair Westerman—or her reaction to him?

Chyenna's phone was giving off a series of beeps. "Batteries need recharging," she said, silently grateful for the brief distraction. "I'll take care of that later." She flipped the switch off and stuffed the phone into her fanny pack.

They made small talk for the next half hour. While she drank her soda and he swigged down his beer, they discussed the weather and the upcoming county fair.

Yet beneath the pleasantries, the casual discourse, the tension that loomed between them sizzled.

"You married, Chyenna?" Blair asked.

"No, not anymore. I got divorced about a year ago. How about you?"

"Nope. I'm single again and intend to stay that way. Martha, my wife, died. About a year ago too."

"Oh. I'm sorry. So sorry . . ."

He jerked his gaze away. "Don't be. I'm not a man who wallows in pity. And don't you go saying anything about it to my little daughter either. We make a point of not talking about it."

"I see." Taken aback by his harsh response, she got to her feet, wracking her brain for a quick excuse to leave. "Well, thanks again for returning my cell phone. I'd hate to be stuck here without it."

"Expecting a call?"

"Yes and no. For now, let's just say no news is good news. I told my business partner, Nan Woodall, I'd keep the phone turned on so she could reach me if she needed to."

"What's the name of your business?" He rose too.

"The Stagecoach Inn, the restaurant formerly run by the Baxton family." She paused. "I've signed a six-month lease with the Baxtons, and when the time is up in October and I've had ample chance to test the waters, I'll have first option to buy."

His eyes widened . . . with what? Surprise? Anger? She couldn't be sure. "Oh, yes! I know all about your little trendy operation. Matter of fact, you're practically my neighbor." But the tone in his voice was anything but neighborly.

"Your neighbor!"

"That's right. Our ranch is the Lazy Y. The property line borders yours."

Chyenna's stomach somersaulted. She didn't know whether to laugh or cry. While all the other businesses in Prairie Valley were clustered typically in the heart of the small town, the Stage Coach Inn was indeed the one exception. Situated about two miles south, it was surrounded by ranches and farms that raised everything from wheat to sheep and cattle.

"Tell me something, lady," he drawled. "Do you happen to take time out from your busy schedule to read the newspaper?" His voice dripped sarcasm. "Or are you so busy trying to change Prairie Valley into another Portland, you don't even bother to know what's going on in our little town?"

"Of course I read the newspapers! And no, I'd never dream of trying to change Prairie Valley into another Portland!" The nerve of this man! How could one man be so arrogant?

"Then perhaps you noticed the editorial I wrote in last Wednesday's edition."

"That was *you*?" Indignation stiffened her spine. "*You* condemned my attempts to attract tourists?"

"Sure thing."

Her face flushed, not only from the heat of his unwavering stare, but for having allowed herself to be caught off guard this way. "But why?" she asked. "I don't understand."

"I thought you said you read it."

"I did . . . but . . . but it's so appalling to me how you'd put down what I'm trying to do, especially the opportunity for progress! Why, surely you—a long-time resident—must realize Prairie Valley is practically withering on the vine. What the town needs is increased revenue. Growth. Plus people with new vision to see that it happens."

"In other words, another big city," he put in dryly.

"No, not at all. A dying community can still survive, still grow without becoming a huge metropolis. That's exactly what it's going to take, Blair. The work of people like myself who want to see places like Prairie Valley survive."

"That depends." He impaled her with a caustic gaze. "That depends, lady, on how you look at it. Most of the folks in these parts are happy with the way things are. We don't need or welcome any blasted outsider's idea of progress."

"But what about the community swimming pool that might have to close due to lack of funding?" She could feel the blood pounding in her head. "What about all the kids who'll no longer have the opportunity to take summer lessons or simply hang out there during open swim sessions? Or all the shop owners that have had to close down and move to bigger towns to simply survive? The citizens of Prairie Valley can no longer afford to keep closed minds, Blair Westerman. It's editorials like yours that help foster shallow thinking!"

"We don't need to do anything to attract more outsiders," he repeated. An artery in his neck pulsed. "There're already too many who're snatching up the land—and all that growth will spoil our wide open spaces, pollute our dark skies, making amateur astronomy almost a thing of the past. Besides, the kids'll always have the old swimming hole down at the river—that is, if all the extra people don't pollute that too."

"Well, I can see you've certainly got your mind made up!" she huffed. "For someone who's supposedly into the all the latest scientific discoveries, your unenlightened attitude certainly doesn't make any sense."

"Don't think of yourself as some small-town savior, *Ms.* Dupres." He was standing much too close, invading her space. And his hot breath against her cheek sent her senses reeling. "Because the bottom line is, what Prairie Valley needs saving from are arrogant folks like you."

"Good day, Mr. Westerman," she answered stiffly, garnering every ounce of self-control. Talk about the pot calling the kettle black, she silently fumed as she brushed past him and started to leave. He'd actually had the audacity to call *her* arrogant.

Yet talking with him again had left her with a strange, breathless sensation, and she immediately despised herself for such a foolish response. From now on, she'd make darned sure she had no further contact

with this infuriating small-town wrangler. Thank goodness the weekend was more than half over.

"Hey, wait a minute! You still haven't told me what
you were doing in my van? Don't forget, Chyenna, you
owe me," he taunted.

"I was changing my clothes, that's what!" she tossed
back hotly. "Your van looked just like mine. No big
deal—though I'm sure you'd like to make that into one
also!" Her cheeks flamed. Her heart hammered. Darn
the man! Why hadn't he just let the matter drop? Embarrassment exploded into anger. An anger so blatant
she could barely see straight.

"Daddy! Daddy! Guess what?"

Chyenna halted. A girl about eleven—Lisa, no
doubt—ran toward them, blond ponytail flying. Excitement lit her fair-skinned face. And trailing directly behind the girl was her own happy, red-haired daughter.

Chyenna sucked in a deep breath and counted to ten.

"Guess what, Daddy? You'll never believe this. I've
found the coolest new friend!"

"Oh, Mama! Hi!" Mandy chimed in, meeting her
mother's bewildered gaze. "We were looking for you.
Wondered where you'd gone." Her freckled face was
flushed, and wisps of auburn hair poked loose from her
French braids. "I got something to ask you, Mama! Can
Lisa come over to our camp tonight? Can she bring her
sleeping bag and sleep in our tent?" Instantly Mandy's
gaze slid to Blair. She caught her breath. "Wait a
minute! You gotta be kidding!"

"What's the matter?" Lisa asked Mandy, wide-eyed.

"Is this *really* your dad?"

"Of course it's my dad!"

Mandy turned again to Chyenna. "Isn't this the man who made the announcement about our cell phone, Mama?"

"Yes, Mandy," Chyenna answered between clenched teeth. "Don't worry. We've got our phone back now. It's right here in my pack." Remembering her manners, Chyenna continued with hasty introductions.

"So can my new friend Lisa sleep over?" Mandy asked again. "We'll be good. We promise!"

Chyenna shot Blair an uncertain look, but he had averted his gaze.

"Yeah, Daddy? Can I? P-l-e-e-z-e!"

Blair dragged his eyes back. They glinted blue ice.

"All right," he answered gruffly. He cleared his throat again. "Just remember to mind your manners, girl. You hear?"

Blair sat outside his tent atop his cooler, staring into the gathering darkness as he washed down the last few bites of his roast beef sandwich with a ice cold Budweiser.

From someone else's camp, he heard a child cry. Nope, make that a couple of kids' cries, he amended as the sound grew louder. Probably that family with the two little ankle biters who had camped farther down the road. That is, if you could call that camping. They'd set up two playpens right there amongst the rocks and sage, but all afternoon the kids had been whiny and inconsolable. He shook his head. They should have known the desert was no place for babies. There wasn't even a decent space for them to run around.

The toddlers cries turned shrill, then started to subside, but off in the distance came a coyote's answering wail. Soon came more. A chorus, perhaps. Mournful. Wild. Despite the haunting sounds, Blair couldn't help chuckling wryly. If anything could get those critters stirred up, it had to be a baby's cry. The sounds evoked memories of two A.M. feedings, teething pains, middle-of-the-night trips to the emergency room—all those things Martha had been so adept at handling, while he'd felt all thumbs.

But that had never meant he didn't love Lisa. Oh no! He loved her more than life itself, he always would. But sometimes—especially now that he was on his own—she could sure be an enigma. In many ways, Lisa seemed a smaller version of her mother, but the entire time they'd been married, he had never even managed to figure Martha out.

Shoving the memory aside, he tipped his head back and glanced skyward. Good. The earlier clouds had cleared and soon it would be dark. Already Jupiter and Venus had popped out, and so had Arcturus, the bright red star to the south in the constellation Bootes. The wind was finally starting to lie down too, and that would add up to another night of great viewing.

All three telescopes—his three most recent models—were set up in the viewing area, silhouetted against the afterglow of sunset like three silent cannons. Soon long lines of those wishing to take a look through the scopes would be forming.

Not only did he relish any opportunity to share the wonders of the night sky with others, he was always on the lookout for anyone who might be interested in placing an order. And so far this weekend, he'd gotten several. That was good too. The extra income would come in handy, seeing as last summer's flash flood had reduced their head of cattle significantly, and he and his brothers, George and Andy, still hadn't gotten quite back on their feet. Besides, the price of cattle this year was forecasted to drop even further.

But as images of telescopes and cattle paraded through his head, another image kept getting in the way.

Chyenna. Chyenna Dupres changing clothes in his van last night. Man, what a sight that must've been.

He gritted his teeth. Don't be a fool, Westerman. It won't work. No, never in a zillion years. You and Chyenna are like the sun and the moon—and all the technology in the entire universe could never change that.

Chapter Three

It was well past midnight. Chyenna, Mandy, and Lisa—bundled in layered clothing—were sitting cross-legged on a large foam pad, gazing heavenward. Within the past hour or two, they'd counted close to thirty bright shooting stars, which summoned exclamations of wonder from all three of them.

Ever since they'd returned to Chyenna's campsite several hours earlier, the girls had chatted excitedly and giggled like long lost friends. They'd shared a simple supper of bean and cheese burritos, tossed green salad, and fresh fruit, then sipped mugs of hot chocolate. Later Chyenna taught them how to make "no-bake" cookies over the camp stove and now they were helping themselves to handfuls of the chocolatey morsels.

"Mama and I don't normally eat much sugar,"

Mandy said to Lisa. "But tonight she says it's okay. It'll give us extra energy to stay up past our bedtimes, so we can watch more stars come up in the east."

"Back on the ranch, my grandma always makes lots of steaks and hamburgers and mashed potatoes with gravy," Lisa replied, licking her fingers. "And she always insists I'm in bed by nine, even in summer, so I can be up early to do my chores."

Eavesdropping, Chyenna could only frown in contemplation. It was no surprise about Lisa's typical diet, of course. Several of the ranchers that had paid their first speculatory visits to her restaurant hadn't hesitated to tell her that the "light" entrées and vegetarian menus fell sadly short of their expectations. Still, the tourists were coming in increasing numbers and word-of-mouth publicity was beginning to pay off. Then too, thank goodness, there was a goodly number of locals who had already become regulars—those who had apparently chosen to dismiss Blair's editorial and patronize the inn anyway.

"So how early is *early*?" Mandy asked between bites.

"Five in the summer. Six the rest of the time when I go to school." Lisa heaved a huge sigh, then continued. "When Mom was around, I had to do chores too, but she didn't make me get up so early." Lisa sighed again. "Grandma's always so busy, cooking lots of stuff for Dad and my uncles and the ranch hands. She also says that the men's he-man appetites have to come first, and when they get around to eating their dessert, they want he-man stuff like cobblers and pies and cakes."

"Gee, Lisa," Mandy said after a long, contemplative pause. "That must be horrible not having your mother anymore."

Obviously Lisa had already told Mandy about her mother dying and their life in L.A., Chyenna decided, her heart turning over in sympathy for the girl.

"Yeah, it's worse than anything you could ever imagine."

"After my grandma and grandpa were killed in a plane accident," Mandy said, "Mama and I used to talk about all the wonderful things we used to do together. Mama and I sometimes talk about them and look at old pictures, too, to help ourselves remember all the special times. Mama says that's what really counts—remembering and talking."

Lisa's voice softened. "My dad won't talk about Mom hardly at all. He doesn't want me to either."

"Why not?"

"I dunno. He just doesn't. He always says some things are better left unsaid."

Chyenna got to her feet and measured out coffee for the camp percolator. She did all she could not to take Lisa in her arms and tell her her father was wrong. *So very wrong.* But that wasn't her place, to undermine Lisa's faith in Blair that way, she quickly reminded herself. It was bad enough the child had lost one parent.

Last thing she needed was to lose all confidence in the only parent she had left.

"Lisa," Mandy ventured. "Let's play a game!"

"Okay! What?"

"If you had three wishes, what would they be?"

"First, I'd ask to have my Mama back. But since that can't happen—and Daddy always said we shouldn't waste time wanting what we can't have—I'd wish my llamas would dance."

"What?" Mandy asked, scratching her head.

"I have these three llamas, see, and I learned at my 4-H club when we were studying llama behavior, that once in a while—but not very often—llamas will dance. The scientific name for that is pronking."

Mandy giggled. "Pronking? That's a silly sounding word. How many llamas do you have?"

"Three. Dancer, the white one, is my 4-H project, and I'm gonna show him at the fair this year."

"Cool!" Mandy exclaimed. "So what's your next wish? You've got two more left, you know."

"I'd also like a kitty that could come inside our house, but Daddy says the barn cats should stay right where they belong—where they can catch mice and earn their keep, whatever that means. Our pet dog, Rusty, got to be inside part of the time, but he died last year."

Chyenna frowned again. Lisa certainly hadn't hesitated when asked about wishes, and so far, they centered around animals. That wasn't too surprising, given the fact she'd grown up on a ranch. But one small kitten inside the house? How could her father object to such an innocent request?

"Mama and I own a kitty," Mandy murmured. "An all-black one that likes to curl up in front of the big fireplace where we live above the restaurant. Sometimes she sleeps on my bed too."

"What's your kitty's name?" Lisa asked, her voice tinged with longing.

"Ebony."

"Cool. I like that name."

Mandy grinned. "Yeah, and I was the one who thought it up. So what's your third wish, Lisa?"

The girl thought for a moment, biting her lower lip. "I wish my daddy could spend more time with me. But of course, except for special weekends like this, he can't. He's got our ranch to run . . . he and my Uncle George and Uncle Andy, of course. And at night Daddy works in his shop, building telescopes."

"Well, at least you get to *live* with your daddy," Mandy answered with grown-up practicality. "We don't even know for sure where mine is. Mama says she thinks he skipped the country."

At the sound of her daughter's words, Chyenna grimaced. Though she and Mandy had talked often about the divorce, it still cut to the quick to hear Mandy talk about it.

The rustle of footsteps intruded upon her thoughts. Chyenna spun around.

"Just thought I should check on my girl," came a familiar voice. "Wanted to make sure she wasn't taking a chill."

"Oh, Daddy! Hi!" Lisa shrieked. She scrambled to her feet. "Mandy and I've been having so much fun, we haven't even *thought* about the cold. Do you wanna no-bake cookie, Daddy? Mandy and I made them all by ourselves . . . well, with just a little help from Chyenna. It was easy! And they taste so good!"

"No. No thanks, Lisa." He shoved his hands into his jacket pockets. "I just took off for a few minutes to see how you're doing and give you your winter jacket. Your grandmother would have my hide if I let you come back sick."

"Honest, Daddy! I'm perfectly fine. I'm wearing two T-shirts and my leggings beneath my sweats. And see? I've got my hat on too, just like you said."

"Put this on anyway." He held out the jacket.

"All right." Lisa sighed.

While Blair's daughter shrugged into the jacket, Chyenna stood up and faced him squarely. She saw the outline of his prominent forehead, deep-set eyes and strong, square jaw. A coil of desire spiraled through her.

"I assure you, Mr. Westerman, I have no intentions of allowing your daughter to become ill or get frostbite. I've extra blankets in my van, and the girls are keeping their insides warmed with lots of hot chocolate." She gestured toward her thermos. "Care for some coffee?"

"Yeah, don't mind if I do." She thought she detected

a hint of mockery in his voice as he added, "Just as long as you don't give me that fancy, espresso stuff like you serve in your diner."

"Nothing but plain black Java, Mr. Westerman," she answered between clenched teeth. His clean male scent enveloped her, disarming her, at the same time making her wish she could take back her offer. It was admirable that he'd wanted to check on his daughter, she decided, but at the same time his presence only stirred another escalating battle within her. Why couldn't he have stayed back in the viewing area where he belonged?

"And by the way," he said, yanking her from her thoughts, "I asked you to call me Blair. Or maybe you've forgotten."

"Fine. Blair it is." Avoiding his steady gaze, she twisted open the thermos with one swift movement, then poured the coffee. Steam curled against the frigid night air as she handed him the mug. For a fleeting moment, their bare hands touched. The brief contact sent tingles of electricity coursing through her.

"Guess what, Daddy?" Lisa exclaimed.

"What, darlin'?"

"We've been making up stories about the stars! It's been so fun!"

"You don't say?" He gave a gruff laugh. "I'm glad to hear you're having a good time, Lisa, but wouldn't it make a little more sense if you girls headed over to the telescopes and learned something useful?"

"Oh, pooh! You're always wanting me to do all that

boring stuff. I'd rather tell stories with Mandy and her mom."

"Mama, Lisa and I are gonna walk over to the porta-potties now, okay?" Mandy interrupted. "I know the way this time. You don't have to go with us."

"All right, Mandy. Just come straight back. Remember not to talk to strangers, and don't get lost."

"Oh, Mom! Why do you keep treating me like a baby? This afternoon, Lisa and I went all around here and we didn't get lost."

"But nighttime's different."

"Don't worry. We'll take our red flashlight. And we promise not to talk to anyone." That afternoon after returning from Blair's campsite, Chyenna had rummaged through her makeup case and found an old bottle of dark red nail polish. Using it, she painted the face of her flashlight, hence doing away with the need to drive back into town to buy taillight repair tape.

"Kids!" Chyenna exclaimed with a soft laugh after the girls had scampered off.

He nodded. "If you're worried about your daughter's safety here, I can assure you that astronomers are probably the safest people in the world." He took a sip of coffee, then grinned at her and added, "Next to cowboys, of course."

She ignored his attempt at wry humor. "Surely you can't blame me for being cautious. Where I come from, kids have been abducted right off their school grounds, sad to say. And besides, my concern isn't any more so-

licitous than your concern about Lisa getting frostbite. . . ."

"No, I can't argue with that." He cleared his throat,
but his voice was husky nevertheless. "Actually, I had
more than one reason for stopping by."

"Oh?"

"Yep." He hunched his shoulders. "I . . . uh . . . I
wanted to apologize. I was rude. Not just this afternoon, but last night too. Not that I'm backing down
from what I wrote in my editorial, mind you. I still stick
by every word. It's just—" he hesitated, "—it's just that
I know better than to talk that way to a lady." He
cleared his throat again. "Despite whatever first impres-
sions you may have about me, I'm really just a country
boy. Born and raised, as I already said . . ." He was still
standing too close. His nearness was pulverizing.

"Apology accepted." She struggled to feign indiffer-
ence, but the hesitation in her voice betrayed her. "I
guess the least we can do is act civil toward each
other—for the girls' sake, of course. "And since you
obviously have no intentions of becoming one of my
customers, we'll most likely not be seeing each other
anymore, anyway."

"Right. Except for the annoying fact that we *are*
neighbors," he reminded her.

"That doesn't mean we can't mind our own business."

"This is Prairie Valley, ma'am," he drawled, "not the
big city. Around these parts, everyone knows his
neighbors."

She held her tongue, refraining from pointing out the obvious fact that since they hadn't neighbored before now, there was no reason they should expect to from here on in.

He glanced around. "Uh . . . mind if I sit down?"

"Suit yourself."

He lowered himself onto one of two lawn chairs. She sat down on the other one, toying with a button on her fleece-lined coat as her thoughts spun. Here she was on this desert mountaintop on what would've been her tenth wedding anniversary, trying to escape the pain, the memories. So how in the world had she happened upon this gorgeous cowboy who was chipping away at her every resolve with each passing moment?

"Tell me about your ex-husband," Blair said without preamble.

His directness caught her by surprise. "Daniel? Why?"

"No reason in particular." He shrugged, staring straight ahead. "Just thought I'd ask."

She drew in a deep breath. "Well . . . Daniel is six years older than myself, and where he's living now, no one seems to know for sure. His big goal in life—at least the way I saw it—was to claw his way up the corporate ladder no matter how many toes he stepped on to get there. We met at a silent auction in Portland, one of those charity fundraisers where all the local movers and shakers like to hobnob. How I ever ended up there, I'm still not certain, but anyway, I did."

"And it was love at first sight?" Blair prompted.

"Yes. Practically." She twisted a strand of hair around her index finger. "Daniel was very good-looking and worldly wise, perfect in every way. Looking back, though, I think I may have idolized him more than really loved him."

"Oh? What make's you say that?"

"Because I never took the time to know who Daniel truly was. I was simply blinded by everything I saw on the outside and before I realized it, I married him." She gave a humorless laugh. "How the relationship lasted as long as it did, I still don't understand. But after it ended, everything I'd idolized in him suddenly came crashing down." She paused, wondering whether she should go on, tell him about Daniel's affair, but decided against it. After all, she was barely acquainted with Blair Westerman. Intimate details were really none of his concern, and she'd already told him far more than she'd intended to.

"Sometimes things change," he said, his voice void of feeling.

"Yes. How true."

A long, awkward silence hung between them. She wished he would leave.

And she longed for him to stay . . .

"I hope my girl hasn't been too much of a problem," he said gruffly.

"No. Not at all. Lisa is more than well-behaved," she answered. "She's a model child. And we've been having such marvelous fun, all three of us."

"Good." He dipped his head momentarily. "She misses her mother, you know. She misses her a lot."

"I can tell that."

"She talked about her?"

"Uh-huh, a little. As much as she dared . . ." Chyenna hesitated. "Mr. Westerman . . . er, Blair?"

"Yes ma'am?"

"I . . . I don't mean to get too personal, but there's something I can't help wondering about . . ." She hesitated again.

"Go ahead." She detected a hint of amusement in his voice as he added, "Don't worry. I won't bite."

"Earlier this afternoon, you told me not to talk to Lisa about her mother. Why?"

He looked down, kicking at a tuft of sage with the toe of one boot. "Past is past. There's no use stirring up old memories. A rancher's life involves hard work, long hours, and sheer determination, with no time to dwell on things that can't be changed, and the sooner Lisa learns that the better. Besides, the last thing I want to do is raise a kid who wears her heart on her sleeve."

"But Lisa's just a child. She's only eleven. It's important she remember her mother and talk about her feelings. That's the only way she'll heal."

"Easier said than done . . ."

"Because maybe you haven't really dealt with your own feelings first."

"My feelings have nothing to do with it," he retorted angrily. "It's just that—"

"Hey, Mama! Mr. Westerman!" Mandy called out as the two girls returned. Their red flashlight bobbed through the darkness, its beam growing larger. "Did you guys see that awesome shooting star a minute ago? It was the biggest one yet!"

Chyenna glanced back in Blair's direction a mere second before he'd jerked his eyes away. She could've sworn he had just swiped away a tear.

Blair gripped the steering wheel as he wended his way down the dusty mountain road. In the back, buckled in her seat belt, Lisa slept soundly. The kid was exhausted, but in a contended sort of way, he suspected. Ever since she'd met Chyenna and Mandy, the weekend had turned completely around. Till then, she'd been whiny and bored. But not so afterward. She and Chyenna's girl had taken to each other like a fly does to fly paper . . .

Lisa had nearly turned cartwheels for joy when she'd learned that she and Mandy were practically next door neighbors. Funny thing, maybe he'd kept his little daughter so busy doing chores, she'd never had time to notice the girl coming and going with her mother. Matter of fact, neither had he . . .

He swerved to avoid a pothole, focusing more intently on the roadway ahead, then let his mind drift back. He had to admit, he was intrigued by Chyenna's warmth, her spontaniety, her enthusiasm—not to mention her physical appeal.

And though she'd come from the city as had Martha—and undoubtedly would end up going back—there *were* differences. For starters, he'd never seen Martha wear a pair of Levi's. Not once. Not even during the time they'd lived on the ranch. Linen and woolen slacks, silk blouses, and expensive tailored suits—that had been Martha's way.

Then too, while he'd overheard Mandy tell Lisa how much Chyenna loved working in her flower and herb garden, Martha had barely known the difference between a rake and a hoe. She'd often said she didn't like dirt under her fingernails, dreaded the prospect of meeting up with an earthworm or worse, a snake. And though his love for Martha was perhaps stronger the day she died than the day they'd married, he'd nevertheless wished she could've let her hair down and learned to love country life—just a little.

He came to a narrow bridge that crossed the slow-running Snake River, his thoughts still spinning. Now that he'd actually gotten to know Chyenna, he regretted having written that piece in the paper. Well, maybe not regretted what he'd said, but more so the way he'd said it.

Yep, let those fool city folk stay right where they belonged, he silently reaffirmed. They had no feeling, no respect for the land and the struggling plight of the ranchers. Why, even when the hunters came every fall, they trespassed on his property, left open his gates, sometimes even shot his cows and tried to make out like it was all an accident. Then, too, there was the extra time and expense rounding up the displaced cattle. Some of his buddies down at the cattlemen's association had even resorted to renting whirlybirds to spot their own lost critters.

The Sunday afternoon sun blazed down, reflecting off the hood of his dusty white van. Off to the side stood open groves of pine with dried needles blanketing the ground. He inhaled deeply, but was barely aware of the woodsy scent as he glanced again in the rearview mirror at his sleeping daughter.

He knew he should be spending more time with Lisa. Maybe even take her back to L.A. and a whirlwind tour of Disneyland, then to the beaches of southern California. But no, he'd never take her back to that godforsaken snarl of people, pollution, and crime. Not in a million years. Besides, there was so much work to do, trying to keep the ranch in the black.

Slowing at a cattle crossing, he drove over it, felt and heard the grates beneath his tires. Soon he had turned onto the main highway that cut through a wide sweeping prairie peppered with cattle. Beyond, the rolling brown hills painted a stark picture against the cloudless horizon.

Unbidden, his thoughts rolled back to Chyenna. Why couldn't he get her out of his mind? But now thoughts of her were no longer gentle, but provocative.

"Maybe you haven't dealt with your own feelings first . . ." she'd accused him.

The memory seared now like a festering wound, burning deeper. The nerve of her, suggesting he was avoiding the reality of Martha's death, plus avoiding Lisa too. Who did she think she was? Some damned therapist? Chyenna had definitely struck a nerve, but he had to admit, if only to himself, it *had* got him thinking. . . .

Yep, the lady had spunk all right. Nerve and spunk and class all rolled into one.

Monday morning dawned sunny, ushering in another scorching summer day in Prairie Valley. By eight, Ernie Paulson, the portly middle-aged post master was sorting mail in the back room at the post office on Main; Harry Mossier was pumping gas at the family-run Jackpot Service Station; and Lucille Allrich was unlocking the cash box at the Shop & Save, the only grocery store in town.

Down the highway, a couple miles out, stood the rustic, two-story Stagecoach Inn. Outside, scarlet geraniums and periwinkle blue lobelia grew in the matching whisky barrels that flanked each side of the wooden steps leading onto the covered front porch. Near the graveled parking lot stood an old covered wagon, one said to have carried pioneers over the Oregon Trail. The inn was constructed of weathered gray shakes where ruffled white tie-back curtains graced the paned front windows. The family quarters took up the entire upstairs, giving Chyenna and Mandy more than ample space to live.

Inside the large L-shaped kitchen that adjoined the restaurant, Chyenna was now grinding fresh coffee beans for the espresso maker. A handful of customers breakfasted at small round tables covered with red-and-white checkered table cloths.

Back now to her ordinary work-a-day world, Chyenna's encounter with Blair Westerman seemed like a mere dream. An eon ago. Almost as unreal as the life she had once led back in Portland, she thought, as she flipped on the switch and the whir of the blades melded into her thoughts.

Off to one side, Nan Woodall was frosting the next batch of freshly baked cinnamon rolls and humming softly as she worked. Nan, a portly, good-natured woman in her mid-fifties, had answered Chyenna's "Help Wanted" ad almost the minute the paper had come off the press. The woman had worked at the local bakery for twenty years before it finally went out of business, and could whip up a batch of cinnamon rolls—the inn's only calorie-laden indulgence—in the blink of an eye. Soon Nan and Chyenna were not only co-workers, but the best of friends. She also shared Chyenna's views unequivocally about the need for new growth in Prairie Valley.

"Mama, did you remember to buy more salt last week?" Mandy poked her head through the kitchen door and grinned, exposing a missing front tooth. While Chyenna and Nan had been busy with the early morning baking, Mandy had set about refilling salt and pepper shakers.

"Yes, there's more salt on the bottom shelf in the pantry," Chyenna replied as she returned her daughter's smile. "Three new jars, as a matter of fact." Despite repeated applications of sunscreen last weekend, Mandy looked as red as a lobster, though she had never complained once. All she could talk about during the hour's drive home was how much fun she'd had with her new friend.

She'd also pleaded with Chyenna to invite Lisa over for more sleepovers, which had posed a new complication. Seeing Blair's daughter again would undoubtedly mean seeing him, too, at least briefly.

But how could she refuse Mandy's innocent request? She couldn't.

After Mandy had disappeared again, Chyenna told Nan about meeting Blair at the Star Party and how he'd informed her it was he who'd written the editorial.

"Doesn't surprise me," Nan commented as she punched down a mound of bread dough and started rolling it out.

"Those Westermans have lived in this valley forever, are tied firmly to their roots. And they don't think twice about letting you know where they stand."

"Did you ever meet his wife?" Chyenna avoided Nan's eyes as she struggled to sound indifferent.

"Martha?"

"Yes."

"Only once when I was paying a visit to the jewelers in town. I went in to shop for a wedding gift for my youngest niece a few years ago and came across her there. Seems she was getting an appraisal on a couple of diamond rings, at least two carats each, I bet. She looked like a British princess getting ready for tea. She was simply beautiful. But I still could never quite figure how she and Blair stuck together—beyond the physical attraction, of course. They were so different from each other.

"Yes, I can imagine. He's deeply affected by Martha's death," Chyenna replied. "He won't even talk about it much."

"Such a pity. For that little girl of his too. I'm sure Blair really did love Martha—if he hadn't, I doubt he would've agreed to up and move the way he did. That shocked the ever living daylights out of this entire town, let me tell you. We never dreamed we'd see the day when any of those Westerman boys would sacrifice ranching for life in the big city. Didn't surprise me one bit either when he and the girl turned up here again after Martha passed on."

"And now that Blair's back here to stay," Chyenna picked up where Nan left off, "seems he's more set in his ways than ever. He's convinced that population growth means total disaster—not only a serious threat to the dark skies needed for star gazing, but to the livability of this entire valley."

Nan shook her head, a smile tugging on the corner of her mouth. "Well, I can't *entirely* disagree with him. I've always thought that someday I might want to dabble in amateur astronomy too. But as far as Blair's ideas about outsiders, I think he is missing the mark. He needs to realize that sometimes things can't always stay the same. Time doesn't stand still for anyone, no matter how much we might want it to. Sometimes failure to grow simply means failure to survive, and Prairie Valley is certainly no exception."

Chyenna nodded. "Any problems while Mandy and I were away?"

"Nothing out of the ordinary. Just a few of the hometown cowboys grousing about our microbrewed beers. They insist they want the old fashioned garden variety types instead. Same for their coffee."

Chyenna wiped her hands on a dish towel and sighed. "Sounds like Blair Westerman all over again. Well, at least the weekend's over, and I won't have to deal with *him* anymore. He as much as promised me he'd never set foot in here." She shook her head, then started to go on, but the squeaking of the front door screen stopped her.

She turned to look, then inhaled sharply. Eclipsing the rectangle of sunlight that poured through the opening was none other than Blair Westerman.

Chapter Four

"Mornin', neighbors." Blair touched the brim of his straw Stetson and flashed the two women a crooked smile. He was wearing a cotton plaid shirt with a red bandanna knotted around his neck, hip-hugging denim jeans that molded his muscled thighs like a second skin, and pointy tan leather boots.

"Good morning, Blair," Nan was quick to reply, giving Chyenna a blessed moment to try to calm her racing pulse. Somehow Chyenna had almost convinced herself he would never show up here, just as she had been telling Nan.

"Going to be another scorcher today," the older woman continued. She slanted Chyenna a wry look.

"Scorcher is right," Blair said in a deep voice. "Temperature's supposed to top 103, according to this morning's paper. Close to breaking an all-time record, so they say."

Her eyes locked with his. She pulled them away, struggling against a fresh wave of clashing emotions.

Darn the man! Why didn't he just stay away and let her get back to her priorities? She didn't need any gorgeous cowboys upsetting her life, especially one who obviously had his own agenda—like trying to lure her into his tempting web, all the while intending to drive her out of town.

He lifted the small brown paper bag he was holding. "Seems as if you Dupres women have a knack for leaving things behind."

"What?" Her mind reeled. "What else could I have possibly forgotten?"

"Oh, I'm not talking about *you,* Chyenna." He opened the bag and pulled out a wrinkled T-shirt. "This, according to Lisa, belongs to Mandy. "It's certainly too small to fit you," he added.

"Oh! Thanks!" She laughed nervously. "Yes. That's the shirt with the picture of the comet I bought for her at the vendor's stand."

"Sorry I haven't gotten around to washing it. I'm afraid we're a little shorthanded these days."

"Not a problem. I'll take care of it." She waved a hand in the air for emphasis. "If I had a nickel for every time Mandy brought home some other kid's clothing after a sleepover, I'd be richer than if I'd won the lottery." She suddenly realized she was babbling like an adolescent schoolgirl and clamped her mouth shut.

"Blair, would you care for one of my giant cinnamon rolls and a cup of coffee?" Nan put in. "On the house, of course," she added as she met Chyenna's astonished eyes.

"If those rolls taste even half as good as they smell, how could I refuse? But I insist on paying. You know us Westermans well enough by now to realize we don't accept any hand-outs."

"Oh, yes." She clucked her tongue. "You're proud and stubborn as the day is long, Blair Westerman, just like your daddy and your granddaddy before him."

"Yes, ma'am. Can't break family tradition, now can we?"

While they talked, Chyenna listened quietly, glancing from one to the other. More than ever, she was feeling like the outsider she knew she still was. And why was Nan practically standing on her head for Blair now, when only a few minutes ago, she'd been ranting how he needed to change his ways?

Yet one added glance at Blair—his lean well-muscled build, the sparkle in his blue, blue eyes, his deceptively charming boyish smile—and the answer became instantly clear. His charisma could melt a female's resolve in less than a heartbeat, and though Nan was old enough to be his mother, she was undoubtedly no exception.

Struggling against her own maddening reaction to him, Chyenna turned her back and busied herself refilling a ceramic cream pitcher with half-and-half.

"So how do you take your coffee?" she heard Nan ask him.

"Black, please. And I'd be much obliged if you could give me a cup of the real stuff—house coffee, I guess the yuppie folks call it."

"Black house coffee and one cinnamon roll, coming right up," Nan sang out. "And Chyenna," she added, "it's high time you take a break too. Go sit down with Blair."

"Oh, I really couldn't." Chyenna sent the other woman a meaningful look, but couldn't dismiss the feeling she was losing ground fast.

"Why not?" Nan asked with raised brows.

"Have you forgotten? We've got a reservation for twelve coming in at lunch today, plus three more cherry cheesecakes to get out. The last thing I'd want to do is leave you in the lurch."

"Yeah, and the luncheon party is still well over two hours away," Nan reminded her. "Now get! Both of you. I'll even deliver the goodies right to your table."

In a matter of minutes, Chyenna found herself seated across from Blair in the farthest corner of the pine-paneled dining room. The small round table was dressed with a red-and-white checked cloth. In the center was a bouquet of burnt orange and white zinnias arranged in an antique blue pint-sized mason jar. While she sipped her coffee, and he ate the warm, gooey cinnamon roll, they exchanged cautious small talk. Meanwhile, a steady stream of customers came and went. Each time the door opened, the antique sleigh bells above it jangled.

Lifting his mug to his lips, Blair commented, "You've put in new carpeting and taken out the booths."

"Yes, quite an improvement, don't you agree?"

"Maybe." He shifted his gaze to the mammoth stone fireplace. "And that must be a gas fire. The former owners burned real wood."

"Right again." She needlessly rearranged the salt and pepper shakers, choking back her growing irritation. "Nan and I agreed the convenience justified the change. Neither of us has the time or energy to track down, cut, and haul firewood."

"Nothing like a real fire, to my way of thinking. Besides, if you get short on fire wood, you can always use chips."

"What?"

"Chips! We've got plenty on the ranch. All you'd have to do is holler."

"What are chips?" she asked, throwing caution to the wind.

"Dried cow manure." He winked, then slanted her a crooked smile. "We use 'em all the time."

"That's disgusting!"

He only shook his head and laughed, but she remained stonily silent.

Chyenna still couldn't trust that Blair's only reason for coming was to return Mandy's T-shirt. After all, it was he who had written the editorial slamming her business, criticizing her for attracting tourism. Had he come today in an attempt to scope out the place? To gather more ammunition—or simply to give her a bad time?

Then, too, it was all too apparent that Blair could have his way with practically any woman he wanted. Chyenna couldn't deny the simmering looks he'd been sending her way since he'd first strode inside the inn—but she'd be darned if she let him get to her.

He checked his watch. "Looks like it's time to get back to mending my fences."

"Before you do, Blair, there's something I must ask."

"Okay. Shoot."

"Why—exactly—did you come here today?"

"What do you mean?" He leaned back in his chair and stretched out his long legs, righting his jaw. "I thought it was obvious. Lisa got her T-shirt mixed up with Mandy's."

"I don't mean *that.* You know as well as I do the girls are planning on getting together again soon."

"Yep." He nodded tentatively, pinning her with a searching look. "I believe they are."

"So returning the T-shirt could have easily waited till then." She wanted to melt beneath his steady gaze, those dark pools that were drawing her in deeper and deeper. Snapping back to her senses, she drew in a steadying breath.

"Are you insinuating that I have ulterior motives for showing up here today?"

"And why shouldn't I? It takes a lot of nerve turning up here as if you hadn't the slightest thing to do with that editorial!" She lowered her voice, suddenly aware that several of the other customers were throwing glances their way. "The way I see it, Westerman, either you support my business a hundred percent or stay away. There's no room for hypocrisy in a small town like this, and you should be the first to realize that."

"I do. Absolutely." He stared down at the table. "And since it looks as if we're playing twenty questions, now it's *my* turn."

She steeled herself for what was to come. "All right. What is it?"

"As I said earlier, we're short on help at the ranch right now, and I'm afraid the situation's only gonna to get worse." He cleared his throat. "Last June, Ma went to her thirty-fifth high school reunion and met up with an old flame, Rusty Cooper. Since then, they've been writing e-mails and burning up the phone lines, and now lo and behold, they're making wedding plans."

"How nice," she said, flashing him a sincere smile.

"Yes and no."

"What do you mean?"

"Ma deserves every happiness, and she couldn't be marrying a nicer guy."

"So what's the problem?"

"If they wanted to settle here on the ranch, there

wouldn't be one. The house where Mom's been staying—the one directly behind ours—has plenty of room for both of them. But she says they've decided to live in Rusty's house instead. It's in Kaiser, about a three-hour drive from here." He frowned. "That'll mean Lisa won't be seeing her grandmother as much anymore."

"Ah . . . I get it. Nice for them, but a mixed bag for you."

"Exactly." He pushed back his empty coffee mug and met her gaze. "But the bottom line is, it'd be selfish of us to try to hold her back. She's spent the best part of her life on the ranch, working hard, trying to do her share to keep us from going under."

Chyenna twisted one corner of her white paper napkin. "Have you told Lisa yet?"

"Actually, Ma has already taken care of that, thank God. I have to admit, it'd be hard for me to have to explain to Lisa that she is gonna lose the second most important woman in her life."

"Yes, I agree," she answered, her heart going out to both Blair and his daughter. He was definitely on his own now, she thought. He had no choice but to sink or swim, and she couldn't help fearing the former would win out. "So what's your big question?" she prompted.

He frowned. "I need to ask if you'd be willing to help drive Lisa to and from 4-H meetings. Of course, I'll try to do my part whenever I can, but I'm afraid the biggest part of the burden might fall on you."

"Oh! Is that all!" She sagged with relief, then broke into a quick smile. "Car-pooling is almost second nature to me. Back in Portland, I took my turn driving Mandy and her friends everywhere—or so it seemed."

"The reason I'm asking is because Ma's at Rusty's place all week, and when she gets back, she's going to be tied up with jury duty. Normally, missing 4-H now and again might not be such a problem, but right now Lisa's getting ready to show her llama at the county fair."

"No need to explain further. I'll be happy to help— now and when school starts too. I was planning on driving Mandy anyway." She paused to think, tapping her forefinger against her cheek. "Let's see, Jenny Nelson is the 4-H club leader, isn't she?"

"Uh-huh. How did you know?"

"She and her husband are regular customers," Chyenna answered. "The Nelsons come to dine here nearly every Saturday night. They're among my most steady local customers."

"Oh!" The surprised look on his face gave her a smug, satisfied feeling, but a clamor at the front door soon crushed it.

"Hey, Mama, guess what? You'll never believe this!" Mandy bounded through, breathless, then stopped dead in her tracks when she spied Blair. Her flushed face lit up with surprised delight. "Oh! Hi, Mr. Westerman!"

"Hello there, Mandy!"

Her smile grew brighter. "I thought that looked like

your pickup in the parking lot." She bit her lip, then burst into giggles. "But is that your—"

The front door flew open again, cutting through Mandy's next words, and a middle-aged couple whom Chyenna didn't recognize blustered inside.

The woman's platinum blond hair quivered with indignation as she shrilled, "I demand to have a word with the proprietor here! Immediately!"

The man—a willowy, balding fellow—dressed in an expensive tailored suit, was obviously trying to pacify her. "Now dear, you've brought at least a dozen other shoes on this trip, and if that doesn't suit you, we can always buy more shoes at the next—"

Chyenna bounded to her feet. "How may I help you, folks? I'm Chyenna Dupres, the owner." Her gaze skittered from first the woman to the man. "Is there a problem?"

"My gracious yes, there's a problem!" The woman yanked off her black patent leather shoe, thrust it in the air, heel up, and hobbling on the other foot, shrieked, "Can't you smell it?"

"Now, dear, calm down." The man patted her on the shoulder. "*I'll* handle this." He turned, offered Chyenna a tight smile, and pointed out the window. "It seems you have a few extra visitors whom you may not be aware of and my wife stepped right into the middle of their . . . ahem! . . . in the middle of their calling card."

Chyenna peered out the window to where he was

pointing. Her stomach dropped faster than an aerial torpedo. There, in the middle of her parking lot, stood three black Herefords, looking perfectly at home.

Blair sat on the front porch steps, gazing past the stables, the sweeping fields of alfalfa. The mere sliver of a moon was inching up from behind the outline of the rolling bare mesa that butted up to the east border of the property. Dusky reddish brown against the fading purple twilight. Immense. Stark. *Achingly beautiful,* he thought.

He'd never grow tired of looking up at those hills. No, never. Luckily, some things stayed the same. He remembered the first time he hiked atop that tableland with his father when he was only eight. Though the trek had been rigorous, testing their limits, the sweeping view once they'd reach the top was indescribably breathtaking. Miles and miles of scrubby sage land, craggy gorges and rolling stark hills stretched in all directions to meet the horizon.

What a contrast to the more livable, less steep hillsides he'd spied in other communities where development had encroached. The wall-to-wall rooftops and concrete had seemed as ugly and invasive as an insidious spreading cancer.

Off in the distance, the mournful cry of a coyote punctuated the stillness. Frogs croaked. A cool breeze rippled across the yard, carrying on it the sweet summery scent of the cottonwoods which lined the banks of the creek behind the house. From the marshlands where the alfalfa grew, he could hear the trumpet call of the Sand Hill cranes.

He heaved a sigh. Another day, with all the usual frustrations and triumphs. The elk breaks in the fences were finally mended. The last runaway steer brought back. But when he and his brothers had attempted to start cutting the hay, they'd been interrupted by an unexpected thundershower—brief, but driving enough to get the hay good and soaked.

He glanced back at the sky and spotted Jupiter poking through, just as he had seen it from the mountaintop the other night. Next to the moon, it was the brightest object in the sky. If he only had time to set up his scope again, he'd check out the planet's four moons.

But no time for stargazing tonight, he reminded himself. Thanks to the Star Party and the publicity it'd brought him, he had gotten orders for five more telescopes. The twelve-and-a-half-inch scope with the special optics and drive connectors would be particularly challenging.

Through the screened front door, the sounds of the television drifted outside. Another kids' sitcom, he decided, with Lisa inside, watching it while she ate the peanut butter and jelly sandwich she slapped together to tide her over till supper.

He plucked a blade of grass that poked up through a crack in the steps. He knew it was the easy way out, using the TV to keep his daughter entertained. But other than helping her with her chores, he didn't know what else to do.

He suspected, too, that Lisa was preparing for Ma's leaving in her own odd little way. Three times now he'd discovered her out in the shed, carrying on an animated one-sided conversation with her llama. Yet Lisa's attachment to Dancer seemed more fueled by loneliness than any typical animal bonding, he decided. Ditto for her wanting a house cat.

Maybe this was her way of dealing with her mother's death, he couldn't be sure. After all, it had been Martha's idea they buy a couple of yearlings. Martha had never approved of slaughtering animals—a terrible predicament, for a cattle rancher's wife, he knew—but with the llamas she needn't be concerned about that. Then, too, selling the fiber might help bring in a little extra cash, she'd pointed out, and Blair had been quick to agree.

At the memory, he felt that old familiar ache settle deep into his gut. Yes, Martha had tried to adjust all right, but it just hadn't worked, just as it wasn't gonna work for Chyenna. *Before long, she'll be crying to get back to the city, the theaters, the big fancy stores. Oh, yes, that's exactly how it'll be. . . .*

Chyenna. The picture of her indignant expression the moment she laid eyes on his Herefords in her parking lot gave him pause. He laughed in spite of himself. Why, he couldn't remember the last time he'd seen a woman so whopping mad—or so enticingly attractive.

Not only had the entire fiasco—which was all his fault, she insisted—made a public mockery of her business, the Herefords had also munched down every last geranium in the planter boxes by the front door!

"What's up, little brother?" The screen door creaked, then slammed shut with a dull thud as George wandered onto the front porch.

"Just sitting here thinking," Blair answered.

George was a year and a half his elder, Andy three years younger. Folks often said Blair and George could've passed for twins, though George was practically a tow head and a few inches shorter. Andy, who more resembled their mother, was short and wiry, with dark wavy hair, and was the best bull rider the county had ever seen.

"Thinking about what?" George asked. "Martha?" he added as he sat down on the step next to Blair.

Blair shrugged. "Maybe."

"Hmm." George stared down at the ground contemplatively, and heaved a sigh. "I got a proposition for you, brother."

"Oh?"

"Yep. Sarah's cousin from Idaho is coming to visit her soon, and she's shown me pictures. Melinda, I think Sarah said her name is. Anyway, she's really a looker, man. Never married, about the same age as you. What do you say we arrange a little foursome some Saturday night and go line dancing over in Blakeston?" Blakeston, population 21,000, about forty miles north of

Prairie Valley, boasted not only a new shopping mall, but also a couple of trendy night spots.

Blair cringed. Though he was happy his brother had found the love of his life, he didn't appreciate George's attempts to set him up. Right now he was perfectly satisfied with the casual "no-strings-attached" friendships he shared with the single gals down at Duffy's Grill.

"Forget it, George," he spat out.

"But why?"

"The timing's just not right yet, that's all."

"When will it ever be right?" George asked pointedly.

"I dunno." Silence stretched between them. "Besides, no one could ever compare with Martha," Blair added.

"All right, man. I get it. But I think it's high time you and me finally did some talking."

"What good would that do?"

"It might help get a few things off your chest, brother. That's the only way you're ever gonna get on with your life again, you know. So far," George added, his voice a trifle bitter, "every time I've brought it up, you've told me in no uncertain terms it was none of my business."

"Maybe I don't want to get on with my life," Blair ground out. It sounded childish, he knew. But the last thing he needed now was his older brother's prying, no matter how well intended.

"Ah, come on, Blair. What kind of fool talk is that?"

"Call it what you want, but that's the long and the

short of it." He turned away, fighting the anger, the self-blame welling up inside of him. *Damn it, Martha, why'd you have to up and leave me without the slightest warning? Maybe, just maybe, if only things had been different, if I could've somehow made them different, your dying would have never happened . . .*

"Would *you* want to start over again if you were in my shoes?" he asked. "Especially if you were practically drowning in guilt?"

"Guilt?" George gave a wry laugh. "What have you to feel guilty about?"

"It's all my fault Martha wanted to leave. If I'd have encouraged her more, maybe introduced her to more of the women in town or taken her out dancing or heck, who knows what I should've done different . . . she'd probably be sitting here with me this very minute."

"That's ridiculous! You can't blame yourself!" George shot him with an incredulous look. "How can you say it was your fault? Martha was determined to get back to the city. It was obvious to everyone. Face it, Blair! There was nothing you could've done to change that in her."

Blair shook his head. "I don't think so. I think she would have eventually come around. Maybe much faster than any of us realized." His voice turned stony. "But one thing I *do* know for sure. I don't want to talk about it anymore."

"Okay by me!" George lunged to his feet. "I won't

bring it up again. In the meantime, little brother, you still got Lisa. "Don't leave her out in the cold. She's the only kid you got . . ."

Blair stared unseeingly into the deepening dusk, listening to the screen door slam shut, and George's fading footsteps. *You still have Lisa.* The words seemed to echo in his head. He swallowed back the sudden bitter taste in his mouth. Who was George to talk about how to raise his little daughter? He didn't know the first thing when it came to kids. Now that made two of them telling him how he should act and feel, George and Chyenna both.

Blair raked his hand through his hair, then let out a weary sigh. They didn't know what they were talking about, either of them. And as for himself, it was better to stay locked inside this invisible cage, safe from the world, safe where he could bleed in private and not be scared of getting hurt again. No, not *ever.*

Standing, he stretched, suddenly feeling weary and old. Time to work on the telescopes, he decided. Somehow work always gave him a desperately needed shot in the arm. Yes, work—that blessed, numbing balm that was becoming admittedly more addictive. He'd proved it before and he'd prove it again.

Work—and nothing else—could silence the demons that clawed inside of him.

Chapter Five

"**P**lease, Lisa!" Mandy exclaimed. "It's my turn now to brush Dancer!"

"Okay. Just make sure you're gentle," Lisa answered, handing over the soft bristled brush. "Llama skin is tender and can get irritated."

"Of course I'll be gentle," Mandy said, indignation edging her voice. "Don't forget, someday I'm gonna have my own llama too."

While Mandy brushed Dancer and Lisa continued her litany of llama care advice, the llama twitched his pointy ears and chomped on alfalfa.

Lisa was certainly in a no-nonsense mood today, Chyenna noted as she set down the bucket of fresh water she'd just fetched for Dancer. But considering Lisa was Blair's daughter, maybe that should come as little surprise.

At five that morning, Chyenna and the girls had loaded the fuzzy white llama into the horse trailer she'd borrowed from Nan and driven across town to the county fair grounds. Lisa and Mandy had both vied for Dancer's attention. She definitely needed to buy Mandy her own llama, Chyenna silently resolved—that is, when she could finally get ahead on money. The initial outlay could be exorbitant, and then, of course, she would need to find a place for boarding. Maybe she might ask Blair if he'd be interested . . .

Actually, she and Blair hadn't talked about much of anything since they'd discovered his cows munching her geraniums right smack dab in her parking lot. The very thought of it still made her seethe. Granted, cattle had the right of way on many of the local roads, but that didn't give Blair the right to allow his to wander onto her property, broken fences or not.

This past month, whenever she'd stopped by the ranch to pick up Lisa, Blair had never been anywhere in sight. Each time Chyenna found herself wondering whether that was by coincidence or design. But as quickly as the question popped up in her mind, she'd shoved it aside. Her only purpose for stopping by the ranch was to carpool Blair's daughter, she reminded herself, not to see or talk with him.

Soon her driving Lisa and Mandy to 4-H meetings

had led to other outings: swimming lessons at the community pool, afternoons at the public library, and frequent trips to the Dairy Queen. Though Blair's mother had returned now, she was tied up every day down at the county courthouse. According to Lisa, her grandmother was growing increasingly distressed about her lack of time for the myriad details revolving around the wedding. Still, Chyenna suspected, she was never one to shirk her familial duties.

"Make sure you tell your grandma I'm more than happy to help out," Chyenna had said to Mandy on several occasions. But there was one major drawback. The more contact she had with Lisa, the greater her chances were of seeing Blair again. And that equated playing with fire.

"I'm going to walk around for a while, maybe grab a cup of coffee at the espresso stand," she told the girls. "Do either of you need anything?"

"Just a chance to flirt with that cute guy with the red hair who walked by here a minute ago," Lisa answered with a giggle. She turned to Mandy. "Did you see the cool way he smiled at us?"

"Sorry, Lisa, I'm afraid I can't do much to help you when it comes to boys," Chyenna replied, playfully ruffling the girl's hair. "What I meant, young lady, was do you need a *snack* or anything else for Dancer?"

Lisa shook her head. "I'll be okay. Dad's given me plenty of money to buy junk food."

"And I brought along the peanut butter cookies Lisa and I made yesterday, plus my allowance," Mandy was quick to add.

"Fine then." Chyenna reached for her purse. "I won't be long. I promised Nan I'd get back to help her as soon as I can, but I'll make sure to check on you girls before I leave."

"Oh, Mom!" Mandy cried. "Stop treating us like babies."

"Yeah, we're gonna be fine," Lisa chimed in.

"All right then, you two are on you own—at least for the next fifteen minutes," Chyenna teased. Actually, this was the first time she'd heard Lisa swooning over a member of the opposite sex, but after all, she *was* almost twelve. Still, Chyenna couldn't help but wonder how Blair would react if he'd heard his daughter.

Striding outside, blinking rapidly as her eyes adjusted to the sunlight, she caught the delicious aromas of sizzling frankfurters and crispy elephant ears mingled with the smells of the livestock from the barns. People were milling around, talking and laughing, and she knew that within another hour or so, the place would be packed.

The colorful sights, sounds, and aromas evoked memories of long ago, a time when her parents were very much alive, and the three of them a small, happy family. Over the years, Mom and Dad had taken her to the state fair in Salem at least three or four times.

Something tugged at Chyenna's heart as she recalled

one particular fall day there when she'd been about four. She and her parents had ridden the Ferris wheel together, then afterward they had bought her her first cotton candy. She'd devoured it, loved every pink sugary bite that melted on her tongue instantly, but not without first getting it all over her hands, face, and in her hair.

How she treasured that memory, that picture of a happy little girl with a mother and father who not only loved each other, but loved her very much also. Yet years later after her breakup with Daniel, the memory had given her new insight, new knowledge: sometimes life can be like pink cotton candy, filled with sweet fluffy dreams, which, once consumed, vanish into nothingness.

Not all marriages were made in heaven like her parents', she'd quickly learned with shattering reality. And though Chyenna knew in her heart she would always remain a dreamer, she also vowed that from that time forward, she'd always dream with her eyes wide open.

She came now to the espresso stand, paid for her coffee, then took a long drink. Unexpectedly she spied Blair striding in through the front gate. Her stomach rolled on its own Ferris wheel ride. He looked sexier than ever with his crooked smile and loose swinging gait. How could she stay angry with him when her defenses were vanishing with each passing moment?

She gave a quick wave, though the smile on his face told her he'd already spotted her.

"Mornin' neighbor!" he called, closing the distance

between them. He touched the brim of his hat, his grin growing wider.

"Good morning, Blair." New awareness warred with caution. Seeing the man was like heaven and hell all wrapped up into one.

"Thanks for getting Lisa here by check-in time. I'm afraid I never could've managed it myself."

"You're welcome. I had the impression you weren't coming today," she replied evenly. "At least that's what your daughter seemed to think."

"I wanted to surprise her. George and Andy insisted they could get along without me for a while."

"Lisa'll be delighted."

"I hope so. Though judging from the way she's been talking lately, I suspect she'll be more interested in checking out the boys here than seeing her dear old dad."

"So you've noticed!"

"Couldn't miss."

"Yes, Lisa's growing up all right." The other day, his daughter had asked her for help selecting her very first bra. Figuring he should know that, Chyenna told him.

"She *what*?"

"She wants a training bra."

He gave a loud groan. "Oh, brother! Why didn't she ask *me*?"

"Because you're her father, and she was afraid you'd tell her that buying a bra wasn't necessary."

"Darned right I would!" A smile tugged at the corner of his mouth. "Maybe I *should* break down and get her a house cat after all. Would sure be a whole lot safer than a boy—or a bra!"

"And you're speaking, of course, from first-hand experience?" she teased.

"You bet." His eyes sparkled down at her. "I just may have to tie Lisa inside the barn and not let her loose till she's forty!"

Her laughter joined his as they started walking again. "Well rest assured, Blair, in another couple of years, I'll undoubtedly find myself dealing with the same problems."

"Little comfort that gives me right now," he ground out.

As they passed by a popcorn vendor, she asked in between more sips of coffee, "Did you get the rest of the hay cut?"

"Yep, thank God. After two thunder showers and the swath breaking down, I was beginning to doubt we'd ever get it done." He paused a moment to glance up at the sky. "If our luck holds out and the weather stays dry, we should be able to get it bailed too."

"How much alfalfa do you normally put up?"

"About a hundred and fifty acres—we buy the rest. And before you know it, we'll have to start trailing the cattle back down from the upper ranch. Mule Deer, we call it. My great granddaddy named it that when he first homesteaded the property."

Side-stepping a clown carrying helium balloons, Chyenna's shoulder brushed Blair's arm. She battled against the intoxicating effects of his musky after-shave, his nearness. The sound of the music from a nearby carousel was momentarily silenced by the words of warning shouting inside her head. *Turn and run from him this very minute! Run fast and far before it's too late!*

"You still ticked at me?" he asked after a long silence.

"Nah. I guess everyone's allowed one mistake."

"Only one?" A teasing awareness sprung to his eyes.

Laughing, she answered him, "Well, maybe one and a half."

"So what do you think of the Lane County fair?"

"I love it. I just wish I had more time to stay today and look around better."

"It's been a lot like this as long as I can remember," he said. "Except it's getting a little bigger every year, especially the 4-H displays."

"That's good. I'm hoping to buy Mandy her own llama so she can join the club after school starts." She paused to toss her cup into a trash container. "That is, if we could perhaps work out an agreement for boarding. My property is less than an acre, you know, and I'm planning to expand the parking lot after I buy the inn. But getting back to boarding, I'm willing to pay you the going rate."

He smiled and nodded to an elderly couple who was passing by, then said to Chyenna, "Let's just wait and see. After all, you might not be sticking around here that long."

"I *will* be staying, Blair. I'm determined to make my

new life here work. Besides, I have no other family anymore, nor any other reason to go elsewhere."

"Your parents are gone?"

"Yes." She told him about their untimely plane crash. "And they were very happy," she was quick to add, "completely devoted to each other till the day they died. I guess that's partly why my divorce was so devastating to me. I wanted my marriage to be every bit as successful as theirs was, not only for myself, but especially for Mandy." She chewed on her lower lip, wondering why she was telling this to Blair. She'd already discovered he was the silent, stoic type, and he probably preferred that she be also. Surely he didn't want to hear about the messy details of her divorce any more than she wanted to become emotionally connected to him.

"Speaking of Mandy," Blair said, "she's becoming quite the little farm girl. Yesterday she helped us shear the llamas and milk the goats. Already she can out-milk Charley Owens and Bill Foster, my two newest hands."

"No fooling!"

"I swear on my grandpa's grave."

"And *your* daughter's becoming equally adept in the art of fine dining," Chyenna told him as they weaved their way through a line of people waiting for fresh caramel corn. "She can set a formal table fit for the Queen Mother herself. Plus arrange fresh cut flowers in the blink of an eye."

"Oh really?" His eyebrows shot up. "But tell me how

that's gonna help Lisa learn to whip up swiss steak, mashed potatoes and gravy for all the menfolk here?"

"That, my dear man, she'll have to learn entirely on her own. Mandy and I fix mashed potatoes and gravy just once a year—with our turkey dinner at Thanksgiving."

It felt good, bantering with Blair this way, especially after having caught a glimpse of his darker, more brooding side. Besides, he wasn't really all rawhide and rough edges. Why, only that morning his daughter had let it slip that sometimes during the night when she got up to raid the refrigerator for a snack, she'd found her father sitting at the kitchen table writing cowboy poetry.

"I'm afraid I need to ask another favor," Blair said as they rounded the corner into the llama barn.

"Oh? What is it?"

"The caterer Ma hired for the wedding reception had to pull out at the last minute—something about he mistakenly double-booked for that same date. The guest list numbers about three hundred, but the menu will be fairly basic." He hesitated. "Any chance you might be interested?"

"Three hundred?" She gulped. "Where is the reception going to be?"

"At the grange. It's just down the road from the church and is roomy enough for everyone to really cut loose. Between both Ma's friends and Rusty's, not to mention all the church folks and members of the Cattleman's Association, the numbers stacked up fast."

Her head whirled. Right now three hundred people felt like five thousand! Still, the added exposure in the community would definitely help, she silently reasoned. Even though she was generating more income now than in the beginning, she still desperately needed to increase her profit margin.

"So when is the big day?" Chyenna asked.

"The last Saturday of this month."

She drew in a long breath. "All right. I'll do it."

He must've sensed her hesitation because he was quick to ask, "Are you sure?"

"Yes. I have on-call backup help in addition to Nan, two other women who are available to fill in at the inn whenever I need them. Tell your mother to phone me as soon as she can."

"You got it," he said with a guarded smile. "And Chyenna . . ."

"Yes?"

"Just one more thing. I want to make it very clear."

"Uh . . . sure. What?"

"This was Ma's idea—not mine."

After Blair and Chyenna visited their daughters, they learned that Dancer had won a blue ribbon. The girls were so elated they could barely contain themselves.

Chyenna gave them both one final hug before leaving. "I'm sorry I have to rush off like this, especially given all this excitement."

"I'll come back for Lisa and Mandy later today,"

Blair offered. "I gotta make another run into town any-way. The vaccine I ordered at the Farm and Feed isn't due in till sometime around five, but I do need to get it as soon as possible."

"Thanks." Chyenna sent him a grateful look. "That'll give me the chance to let Nan go a little early tonight."

"Let's plan something special to celebrate Dancer's blue ribbon!" Lisa broke in.

Blair paused, twisting his mouth in contemplation. "Hmm, that's a good idea. How about a trip to the old swimming hole?"

"Oh, Daddy!" Lisa scowled. "Swimming there's gross! Last year in science class, we went there to get water samples. When we got back to school and looked at them under the microscope, we saw all kinds of creepy crawlers!"

"Oh, yuk! I'd never want to go *there!*" Mandy was quick to agree.

"See, Daddy? Besides, Chyenna takes us to the swimming pool all the time."

"Women! I can sure tell when I'm out-numbered."

Chyenna bit her lip to keep from laughing.

"I got it!" Lisa shrieked. "I got the perfect idea! Let's take the llamas on a pack trip! Maybe we could go up to Mule Deer and spend the night in the cabin!"

"Well, now . . . *now* you're talking."

"So when can we go, Daddy?"

He considered for a moment. "Maybe in another few

weeks or so, after we're caught up with the fall chores." Rocking back on his heels, he added, "Besides, school starts in just a few days. You'll want to get on top of your new classes and assignments before you even think about running off on any more camping trips."

"Work, work, work," Lisa grumbled under her breath, folding her arms across her chest and frowning. "All you ever think about is work."

"We *will* go, Lisa. I prom—"

"Can Mandy come too?" She cut him off.

Blair cleared his throat. "Er . . . why, I don't see why not . . ."

"Cool!" the girls chorused, jumping up and down.

"And maybe Mandy's mother might like to join us also," he added quickly.

Chyenna gave an inward groan. While part of her longed to blurt out an unequivocal yes, the other part remained wary.

"I'll think about it," she replied.

"You think long and hard, ma'am," he drawled. Yet the glint in his blue, blue eyes quickly told her he already knew her answer. . . .

Once Chyenna had left, Blair chatted with the girls awhile longer, then decided to look around a little more before it was time for him to leave also.

He checked out the various breeds of cattle, studied a display sponsored by the BLM about forest conservation, then shot the breeze with a couple of buddies from the Cattlebreeder's Association, Billy Nelson and Sam Kudleman.

They swapped weather predictions for the coming winter and commiserated about the current price of cattle.

"Hey, Westerman," Kudleman continued, giving Blair a friendly slap on the back. "I noticed you hitting on that new chick in town, the one who's trying to turn the old Stagecoach Inn into some newfangled coffee bar."

Blair clenched his hands at his sides. "So what of it?" he asked tightly. "You got a problem with good-looking women?" The last thing he felt like putting up with was razzing from his buddies.

"Nope. No problem at all," Kudleman answered innocently, but the sly gleam in his eyes betrayed him. "You know me better than that, buddy."

"And that reminds me . . ." Now it was Nelson's turn. He flashed Blair a cheeky grin. "Whatever happened to you and good old Lucy Bush, that gal we saw you shooting pool with down at Duffy's Grill? This Dupres babe—or whatever her name is—is a bit out of your league, ain't she, man?"

"Now just you two hold on," Blair spat out. He struggled to reign in his temper, but was afraid he was going to lose it. "Don't you go comparing Chyenna to Lucy, because there *is* no comparison!" How had he let himself get backed into a corner like this? Blair wondered miserably. Though he'd certainly dated his share of women, even a few after Martha had died, he was never one to brag about his conquests.

"Yep, good old Luce," Nelson said.

"And before you two fools go getting any ideas, I'll have you know Chyenna's not like Lucy. She's a lady. A real lady. Just like Martha was."

"Say, Kudleman," Nelson continued, ignoring Blair's protest, "have you happened to hear the talk around town? Why, old Charlie Parkinson stopped by the Stagecoach Inn the other day and tried to order a nice cold Bud, and what did she tell him but the only stuff she had on tap was microbrew! Now don't that beat all?"

Both men slapped their thighs and tossed back their heads, laughing.

"All right." Blair squared his jaw, his temper cooling a little. "I'll agree with that much. I like my Bud too. Always have. But the bottom line is, Chyenna's a classy, hard-working gal with a good head on her shoulders. And the only reason you saw me talking with her today was because our daughters are hanging out together." With that, Blair turned on his heel and started to leave. "See you around."

"Yeah, later, man," Kudleman called after him.

As Blair stalked back to the entrance gate, he pulled the brim of his Stetson down a little lower. There was something darned unsettling about what had just happened. Why was he suddenly defending Chyenna, especially when a little over one month ago he was one of her biggest critics? And most of all, why was he making such an effort to downplay the way she was affecting him?

Because it's true that she's a lady, a small voice inside of him answered back. *The lady's starting to get to you, man.*

And that means you'd better watch out. . . .

Chapter Six

The days ticked by into mid-September, ushering in a more tranquil, gentler pace at the Triple Y. The alfalfa had been trucked in, the Herefords pregnancy tested, and vegetable garden harvested, not to mention a myriad of smaller routine chores. Then, too, the girls had started back to school immediately following Labor Day. But for Chyenna, the beginning of autumn also meant dwindling tourism and a dwindling cash flow. How would she ever manage to stay in the black through the winter?

The following Saturday morning as she was flipping buttermilk pancakes in the family quarters for Lisa and Mandy—who by now were practically inseparable—she silently contemplated her plans for the day. This was the first day off she'd had in over a week, and later that afternoon she needed to drive into town to stock up on supplies. But first she and Blair's mother had agreed to meet at the ranch to plan the reception.

"Lisa needs my help worming the llamas," Mandy announced from where they were seated in the sunny breakfast nook. "And after that, we going to spread out the dung piles!"

"Busy day," Cheynna agreed, smiling to herself. It wasn't difficult to understand her daughter's delight over Dancer's blue ribbon, nor her growing enthusiasm for milking the goats, and picking fresh vegetables. But worming the llamas and slinging dung? Now that had to be the mark of a true country girl . . .

"Then later," Lisa said, her words tripping over each other, "we're gonna take the horses and round up stray cattle. Some of the cows come down to the creek to drink in summer instead of staying up at Mule Deer." She washed down a bite of pancake with a gulp of milk and added, "Mule Deer is where all the pairs and the yearlings are now, you know. And Dad says the real trick is keeping them up there."

Not to mention keeping them out of my parking lot, Chyenna added silently with mixed amusement and annoyance.

After clearing the table and rinsing their plates, the girls were soon off. Later, Chyenna, too, was on her way. As she pedaled her mountain bike down the narrow gravel lane, the sweep of the ranch, bordered by a white post and board fence, lay before her. *What an idyllic, homey sight,* she thought with unexpected appreciation—and a pinch of wistfulness.

On either side were fields abundant with wild grasses. As the main ranch house drew nearer, she spied a trim front yard with a juniper hedge and two trellises laden with burgundy-colored roses. Their rich perfume carried on the breeze.

Stopping for a moment, she shaded her eyes with one hand to get a better look. The main ranch house where the three brothers and Lisa resided had a high-pitched dark green roof, three white dormers and covered front porch with what appeared to be wicker furniture.

Behind it stood the smaller home where Blair's mother lived. Lisa had said her uncles used to live there also until she and her parents had left for L.A., at which time George and Andy moved back to the larger home, granting their mother some well-earned solitude.

Off to one side, the creek meandered its gentle downhill course, the same creek that bordered her own small parcel. Beyond stood two corrals, a weathered red barn, and sprawling white stables. Sunlight glinted off their matching metal roofs. A combine droned from somewhere in the distance.

"Your daughter's becoming quite a little farm girl," Blair's words echoed inside her head. No wonder, she decided now, given all the beauty and serenity here, though undoubtedly her daughter was drawn to the ranch for more childlike reasons. And here Mandy was truly free to be just that—a happy, carefree child whose journey into adulthood and its many complexities would come all too swiftly.

As she pushed off on her bike again, she thought back to her own childhood. YMCA summer camp in the country, miles from where she'd grown up in the suburbs of Portland. She'd attended several years and every summer after camp was over, she could hardly wait to go back again.

Without warning, her memories sharpened, came alive. The clean mountain air stinging her face, the woodsy scent of dried pine needles, the sweet sounds of birdsong. Ah, yes, that precious link from the past to the present—weren't these the same delicious sensations she was experiencing this very moment?

Yes, this was what had drawn her here. It was more than the prospect of adventure, a simpler way of life, the need to carve out a livelihood for Mandy and herself. In the beginning after she'd read the For Sale ad in the paper and made her first speculatory visit to the inn, she'd been at a loss to define that vague beckoning. But now she knew. She knew with every fiber of her being. She required that wholeness, that link with the infinite—not simply during a fleeting week at some camp in the pines. She knew now she needed it for the rest of her life.

Chyenna braked at the bottom of the stairs that lead

up to the porch. A movement off to the side of the house caught her eye, then vanished. Who had it been? Blair?

No, you mustn't think about him or expect to see him. Get a grip! Blair isn't the reason why you're here. Besides, it probably wasn't him anyway. He's certainly not the only male working on this ranch.

But as she dismounted the bike and prepared to go inside, all her silent words of warning slipped from her mind.

Sharon Westerman offered Chyenna a chair at the oak kitchen table, then sat down on the other side. They had agreed to meet at the family home instead of her own because she had planned to spend the day there, cleaning.

Sharon, in her mid-fifties, was petite and slender, dressed in form-fitting jeans topped by a champagne-colored blouse. She wore her salt-and-pepper dark hair in a stylish short cut with just the right amount of wave. A far cry from the stereotypical buxom, apple-cheeked farm wife Chyenna had previously envisioned.

"It's so good of you to step in at the last minute like this," she said without preamble.

"I'm always eager to take on a new challenge," Chyenna replied, though if the truth be known she was still quaking at the prospect of three hundred guests. "That's what prompted me to buy my business in the first place—though many of my friends and co-workers back in Portland predicted I could never make a go of it."

"Nonsense," Sharon said with a smile. "As far as I'm concerned, I was more than glad to see a new owner take over the inn and try to make it work. What that place needed was some new blood, new energy, and you my dear, are exactly the right person to have taken that on."

"Thank you." Chyenna hesitated, chewing on her lower lip. She went on to explain the conditions of her lease-option-to-buy, come due the end of October.

"Good luck. I do hope you can stay. My granddaughter, for one, would be crushed if you and Mandy had to pick up and go."

Chyenna forced a hopeful smile. "I know my daughter would feel equally crushed."

Sharon got to her feet and asked, "Would you care for a warm apple fritter? And how about another cup of tea?" A look of frank embarrassment crossed her face. "Or maybe you would've preferred coffee all along. It was rude of me not to have asked first. I hear you serve a variety of wonderful fresh ground flavors at the inn."

"Yes we do, but tea is fine. I'm afraid I'll have to pass on the apple fritters though." She flashed the older woman another smile. "My business partner's home-made pastries have already added an unwanted inch to my waistline."

A moment later, Sharon Westerman returned with a rose-patterned teapot and refilled Chyenna's cup. As Chyenna took a long, slow drink, she savored the fresh, minty taste and scent. Somehow it seemed so fitting, sitting here with Sharon in this lovely old-fashioned kitchen, sipping tea and chatting. Never mind that this was really nothing more than a business meeting . . .

"I want to thank you again for your generous help with Lisa," Blair's mother said, sitting back down. "I know my son appreciates it, too, though sometimes he may be too proud to tell you so."

"I can believe that," Chyenna answered, staring down at the floral pattern of her lemony yellow place mat. She lifted her eyes and met Sharon's thoughtful gaze. "And now that you mentioned it, I'm surprised Blair's pride didn't get in the way of him asking for my help," Chyenna went on levelly.

"Yes, so am I." Faint worry lines creased the older woman's forehead as she lifted one shoulder. "I only wish Blair could be willing to start over as I am, though for him, that could never mean moving away again . . ."

"Yes, he's made that quite clear." Chyenna feared the conversation had moved toward dangerous territory, but she also realized she'd be remiss if she failed to add, "I'm sorry to hear about Martha. It's so tragic for Lisa as well."

"More than tragic," Sharon agreed, shaking her head. "And as I said, I'd give my last dollar if Blair could only meet a nice young woman and settle down. It's not impossible—if only he'd be willing to try." She released a long sigh. "After all, I've been through the grieving, too, and all that goes with it: the denial, the anger, the guilt . . ." She stopped and stared out the window before continuing. "So far, I'm afraid, the only one who's ever succeeded in getting Blair to talk is my eldest son, George, and even at that, it didn't happen till just the other night." Her shoulders slumped. "Later George informed me that he offered to set Blair up with his fiancée's cousin, but Blair got upset about that and insisted he wasn't interested."

Chyenna lowered her gaze and busied herself scanning her notepad. She could feel Sharon Westerman studying her intently, which made her feel all the more uncomfortable. Though Chyenna, a mother herself, could empathize with Sharon's solicitude, Chyenna certainly hadn't come here to discuss personal family matters—especially anything that smacked of Blair's love life.

"Let's see now," Chyenna said, taken aback at the shakiness she heard in her voice, "is there anything else we might've forgotten in regards to the menu?"

"No, I think we've covered everything." It hadn't come as any surprise that Mrs. Westerman wanted a western style buffet, complete with barbecued chicken and ribs, roasted spuds, buttery corn on the cob, molasses baked beans, cheesy corn bread and a spread of deli salads. For dessert, in addition to the traditional wedding cake, she'd opted for cherry cheesecake, having heard via local gossip that Chyenna's low-fat version had indeed earned a four-star rating.

"Oh, and what about beverages?" Chyenna asked. She tapped the eraser end of her pencil against the table.

"I'd like plenty of champagne and at least two punch bowls, one spiked, the other missionary style. There'll be a no-host bar, also, for those who care to order mixed drinks." Sharon Westerman scrawled a note on the steno pad before her, then added. "And we'll need coffee and tea, too."

"Would any of your guests prefer Italian sodas or sparkling water?" Chyenna asked, thinking back to the beverages served at the inn. Though the tourists often ordered these more trendy beverages, a growing number of townspeople were beginning to also.

"Why not? If they don't go over well, and there's some left, Rusty and I'll pack them into the fifth wheeler before we leave on our honeymoon. And oh, that reminds me, why not include some tofu herbed linguine and eggplant parmesan to the entrée menu? You know what they say about variety being the spice of life . . ."

Amazed, Chyenna blinked. "Excuse me? You're saying you want to include two meatless entrées for a crowd of people from primarily the Cattlebreeder's Association?"

"Why not? That's the way Rusty and I eat. Besides, I'd like to make sure there'll be plenty of everything to suit everybody." Pink stained her cheeks as she added in a hushed tone, "Though I can whip up a pretty mean chicken fried steak, if I do say so myself—and cook lots of beef to stay in my sons' good graces. Quite frankly, I gave it up a long time ago."

As Chyenna jotted down the additional items, she smiled to herself. Putting together this reception just might prove more fun than she'd originally anticipated. The more she and Sharon Westerman talked, the more Chyenna admired the older woman's high-spirited demeanor. Besides, who said that meat and meatless couldn't coexist on the same buffet table?

"Ma! Is that you? Is Chyenna there too?"

"Yes, son. Come in. We're just finishing."

Blair walked into the kitchen and flashed them a quick grin. He looked at first at his mother, then Chyenna. His eyes lingered, sending her silent messages.

"Would you like a quick tour of the ranch?" Blair asked her after Sharon had excused herself and disappeared into an adjoining room.

Chyenna stood up and smiled. "Yes, I'd love that!" Though her head was still reeling at his unexpected appearance, at the same time, it hadn't come as a total surprise. Had Sharon Westerman told him about their prearranged meeting?

His hand caught hers as he led her outside to his pickup which was parked beneath the shade of a red barked cedar. She felt his work-roughened palm, the hand of a man who clearly toiled out-of-doors. Yet his touch was like fire—hot and pulsating. Bolts of awareness pounded through her.

"Sorry I can't offer you air-conditioning," he said as he held open the passenger door and waited for her to slip inside. "The van's the only rig that has it, and Andy took it into town about an hour ago."

She smiled over at him. "No problem." As he strode around to the driver's side, she couldn't help noticing his tall, lithe form, his easy gait. When she'd spent time with him at the fair, she been all too aware of the covert, appreciative female glances sent his way. It was a wonder some woman hadn't nabbed him by now—though on second thought, given his penchant for avoiding serious commitments, maybe it wasn't so surprising.

Which was fine with her—after all, she didn't want to get emotionally involved either.

"Where're the girls?" she asked as they started down the dusty lane. So far, she hadn't seen a trace of them.

"I talked with Mandy and Lisa just before I came inside the house," he answered. "They were still over at the llama shelter with George, finishing up the worming." He executed the truck over the deeply rutted lane. Tall blades of grasses slapped both sides of the pickup as they wended their way around the next curve. "We also settled on a date for the pack trip I promised them."

"Oh? When?"

"The weekend of October fifteenth—Lisa's birthday."

"Good idea."

"Yeah. I hope so." He grew quiet for a long moment before adding, "You are planning to come, I hope . . ."

"Uh . . . well . . . I don't see why not." She'd go for Lisa, help make her birthday special, she silently vowed. After all, this was only her second birthday without her mother.

"George is gonna tie the knot, sometime next spring," Blair went on, changing the subject.

"So that'll leave just you, Lisa, and Andy . . ."

"Yep." He gave a wry laugh, yet Chyenna hadn't mistaken the faint yearning in his voice, an inference that he was feeling all the more abandoned.

The roadway led to a narrow wooden bridge that spanned the creek. Beyond stood the bunkhouse.

"Your property seems to just go on and on," Chyenna said, duly impressed. She tilted her head. "When did you say you bring the herds down from Mule Deer?"

"Usually around the first of October, depending on how early the snow starts to fly. We haul them in trucks, usually our own, though sometimes we rent semis." The first stop was the stables with its airy stalls and the wooden stairway that led to the loft. The sweet scent of hay drifted from open bins.

Next came a large corral where two russet-colored Tennessee Walkers grazed. Beyond, three milk choco-late colts frolicked, their silky manes whipping in the wind, while a black stallion with a white star on its forehead trotted over to where Chyenna and Blair were standing.

"That must be Shadow," Chyenna said with a grin. She shaded her eyes to see better. "My daughter tells me Shadow's her favorite."

"Yep. She's the only black horse we've got now. Her mother was black too, but we lost her last year."

"Ah . . . it's a wonder you didn't name her Black Beauty." She could understand now how Mandy had taken to the horse so.

Blair reached into the pocket of his denim jacket and extracted a small apple. "Here. Want to feed her?"

"Oh yes!"

He showed Chyenna how to make a flat palm, then handed her the apple. In no time, Shadow had chomped it down. Then she nuzzled Chyenna's hand, searching for more. Her snout felt warm and dry.

"Sorry, old girl," she said, laughing. "Next time I'll come better prepared."

Next time! She stopped herself. What made her think there would *be* a next time? Blair had simply offered her a quick look around. Except for the upcoming pack trip, she'd have no reason to set foot on the ranch again.

Blair was quiet for a long moment, then finally spoke. "I decided this morning to definitely let Lisa have her kitten. In fact, I'm gonna try to catch her right now. Want to help?"

"Of course! I think she's got her heart set on the tabby with raccoon markings."

"Right." He pushed back the brim of his Stetson, then fished out a pair of leather gloves from his jacket pocket. "Only problem is, those barn cats are so darned wild. I've got an old fish net out in the storage shed behind the bunk house. If worst comes to worst, I can always fetch that too."

A short time later, they found the tabby in the hayloft, pouncing on insects, batting at fluttering moths. Yet whenever they got even remotely close to her, wide-eyed and quick as lightening, she darted away.

Chyenna dissolved into fits of laughter as she watched Blair, skulking about on hands and knees, bits of hay clinging to his T-shirt and in his hair, the fishnet poised and ready.

"Blair Westerman, I think you've finally met your equal," she teased from where she was sitting on a bale of alfalfa.

He slanted her a boyish grin. "Ah, to heck with this! I'll think of something else . . . later." He set down the fishnet, then joined her.

She tipped back her head, looking up at the rafters. Spider webs and a couple of water stains lay directly above them. "Have you ever seen bats up there?"

"On occasion, but they're really not as ferocious as folks make them out to be. And unless they're rabid, they don't normally come out during the day."

She lolled her head to one side. "Well ferocious or not, I don't intend to meet up with any."

"Then just make sure you don't hang out in any haylofts at night," he teased, settling back also. His voice turned pensive. "I remember when my brothers and I were kids. Sometimes we played hide and seek here after chores were done. The hay made perfect hiding places. But often at night, I'd come here alone. One early fall night when I was ten or so, I was lying here on my back and looking straight up through a hole in the roof . . . I can't remember now just why it was there, but anyway, it was. I liked to pretend that the barn, especially the loft, was my own secret observatory—without a telescope, of course."

Darting him a sideways glance, she smiled, nodding.

"That particular night," he continued, "I spotted this fuzzy oval patch, not quite the size of a full moon, but much, much fainter."

"A UFO?" She chuckled.

His laughter melded with hers. "No, though on first glance, that question crossed my mind too. But anyway, I was fascinated by that object, and the next day I pleaded with Ma to take me to the library in town, so I could get my hands on an astronomy book. I learned it was called the Andromeda galaxy. After that, I would come every night and lie in this very spot, staring up through that hole. It blew me away to think I could see another spiral galaxy so much like our own without even using binoculars. Sometimes I wondered if there was a kid somewhere up there like me, looking back at our Milky Way . . ."

She smiled again, picturing him as a young boy, freckle-faced with wheat-colored hair and perhaps a cowlick or two. She was touched, hearing Blair open up this way to share a small part of himself.

Though so unlike him, it seemed.

She couldn't help sharing too. She told him about summers at the Y camp, the horseback riding and how at night she'd love to stare at the Milky Way. "That, for me, was probably the first time I came to truly appreciate all the wonders of nature. The sunshine and fresh air, the creek where we swam, the forest where we made lean-tos and slept out in them at night, the sense of adventure around every new turn. And I do believe that was part of the reason—at least, on an unconscious level—I was so compelled to pick up stakes and move Mandy and myself here."

"What a romantic you are. Maybe your ex-husband, louse that he was, was just a little bit right about that."

"Yeah. Maybe." Her voice caught. "But I'm not a foolish dreamer. Not anymore."

"No, never," he agreed huskily. In the space of a heartbeat, he'd drawn her close, pulling her into his arms. "Truth is, neither of us are fools. But I can't deny my attraction to you, Chyenna." His lips brushed hers. "And I know you can't either."

She smiled, silently chiding herself for not drawing away.

But she couldn't.

Not yet. His strong masculine arms felt too delicious, his nearness too enticing.

"Admit it, Chyenna. The attraction's growing . . . and no matter how hard we try to fight it, it's getting stronger."

"No, don't say it . . . we're both lonely, that's all."

As their gazes locked and held, she took in the play of shadow and light on his handsomely carved face, his strong profile.

"Blair . . ."

"Hmm?" He gently stroked back her hair.

"It's getting late . . . you're supposed to be—"

"Shh . . ." He angled his mouth down and claimed hers, softly at first, with such tenderness she wanted to melt. His lips felt wonderful. He tasted like heaven a thousand times over.

"Oh, Blair . . ." Her exclamation came on the heels of a sigh. The kiss deepened and took on a new urgency. It played on and on as beams of sunlight slanted in through the loft window. The kitten, long forgotten now, scampered out of sight—as had every last shred of Chyenna's determined resolve . . .

"Daddy! Are you here?"

Chyenna sat bolt upright and blinked.

"Mama! Where *are* you guys?"

Blair straightened, too, and dragged his hand through his hair, emitting a low groan.

"We're up here. In the hayloft!" Chyenna was quick to call down. Brushing the straw from her clothing, she scrambled to her feet and pasted on a smile, though her knees were still as weak as jelly and her heart was racing. "We're trying to catch that kitten you've been wanting," she chirped as she began her way down the loft stairs. Blair waited until she was near the bottom, then began his descent also.

A chorus of giggles from the opened door of the barn pierced the stillness. "Catch the kitten!" Mandy squealed. "Looks like you guys are a little too late! We've already got her!"

"Yeah, and she's *so* cute," Lisa chimed in. "She's got the coolest green eyes and the prettiest pink nose and I'm gonna name her Raccoon." Blair's daughter beamed as she cuddled the young feline against her, smiling adoringly down at it. Suddenly her head snapped up. "But oh, Daddy! There's something important, thàt's why we really came! Grandma said to try to find you as quick as we could!"

"What is it, Lisa?" He and Chyenna were standing in the opened doorway now, facing their daughters while the sunlight flooded through in soft, slanting ribbons.

Lisa gripped the now struggling kitten, her voice urgent. "There's a man from Hollywood with a big fancy car asking to talk to you, Daddy! He's back at the house right now with Grandma."

"What?" Blair asked. "What the—what on earth for?"

"He says he's here on business and he's looking for Mandy's mother too. Hurry, Daddy! Grandma said!"

Chapter Seven

"**M**s. Dupres, Mr. Westerman, I assume." The man smiled and rose from the easy chair where he was sitting in the living room, making idle talk with Sharon Westerman. He wore a red bandanna around his thick head of black hair, cinched back in a ponytail. Inscribed on his black T-shirt were the words "Odyssey Productions."

"Oh, good! The girls tracked you two down!" In a tither, Sharon sprang to her feet, smoothing out her blouse. "I was afraid I was going to have to tell Mr. . . . er, Mr. . . ." she darted a nervous glance in the man's direction. "Oh, my! Already I've forgotten—"

"Clancer. Harry Clancer." He smiled blandly and shook hands while Sharon Westerman made hurried in-

101

troductions. Then Sharon excused herself and hustled the girls off.

"Can't we stay too?" Lisa's voice floated back down the long hallway. "We were the ones who found them, don't forget! And guess where they were?"

"No, child." Sharon's words, a trifle stern, were growing fainter. "Don't you think it's time we make a bed for your kitten to sleep in?" The voices and scuffle of footsteps faded, then a door slammed shut.

"What can I do for you, Mr. Clancer?" Blair asked. He and Chyenna took their places on opposite ends of the white leather couch across from him.

Chyenna felt her shoulders tense. Why was this . . . this Harry Clancer here? Why did he want to talk with Blair *and* her? It didn't feel right. It felt too much as if she and Blair were a couple—or at least business associates, which could be equally disastrous. She shifted again, heard the creak of the leather beneath her. . . .

"Harry. Just call me Harry." The man flicked his gaze to Chyenna, assessing her with obvious interest.

"All right, Harry." Blair gave a curt nod.

"By way of explanation, I happened to stop by the Stagecoach Inn before coming here," Harry continued, still looking at Chyenna. "Your associate—I believe she said her name was Nan—told me you were here discussing business." He smiled again. "Nice dining establishment you've got, ma'am. I stuck around there long enough to eat breakfast, and I might say, those cinnamon rolls are better than any I've found in L.A."

"Why, thank you," she answered, sending him a pleased look.

"So what is it, Harry, you need to discuss with us?" Blair interjected, dragging the man's unwilling eyes back to his own. "The ranch isn't for sale, if that's what you wanna know," he added.

Harry Clancer threw back his head and laughed. "You can breathe easy, my friend, because that's the farthest thing from my mind." He cleared his throat. "The reason I'm here—and what luck to find you both in the same place so we can discuss this at the same time—is because I'm a location scout from Odyssey Productions. The rest of my crew is coming through in a few days, too, but I'm the one who does the up-front legwork." Harry jerked his head toward the back of the house where Sharon and the girls had disappeared. "I spoke first with your mother about my offer, but she said she's turned the ranch over to you and your brothers, and ultimately the decision is all three of yours."

"What decision?" Blair asked levelly. His eyes narrowed with suspicion.

"Perhaps you've heard about the range fire over in Mattillo, near Hell's Canyon?"

"Oh, yes," Chyenna put in. "Isn't that the fire that got started by lightening a few days ago?" She angled a glance at Blair, who was already sending her a grim warning look.

"That's it. We'd planned to start our next production in exactly three weeks. The location shoot is—or I should say was—a lot like what you folks have here, a historic landmark inn and a cattle ranch next to it. Both settings are inherent to the story line, an old-time western set during the late 1800s. The two principle actors are Billy Halligan and Bethany Daniels, both nominees for last year's Academy Awards." He paused, apparently waiting for their reaction, but they only remained stonily silent.

"Odyssey Productions must find another location shoot as quickly as possible," the scout continued a minute later. "We're running out of weather. This is a summer story and already it's looking a lot like fall. We'd like to relocate our shoot to your ranch, Mr. Westerman." He turned to Chyenna. "Plus take several shoots at the Stagecoach Inn also. We're prepared to offer you both a generous sum, especially now that the timing is so critical. And not only would we like to do part of the shoot at the inn, we might be able to work out something extra in the way of support services also. If you'd be willing to provide meals, that—for us—would sweeten the deal even more. Hopefully, it would for you also."

Blair's face suddenly paled. "And exactly how generous *is* this generous sum?"

"A couple hundred grand for the use of both properties. Plus the going rate at the restaurant, with 25% gratuities guaranteed."

Though Blair flinched, his face remained masklike. "I hope you realize, this is asking a lot. Folks around here don't normally take too well to outsiders, much less an entire movie crew."

Chyenna struggled to keep from disagreeing as the scout answered, "Understood, Mr. Westerman."

"I'll need a little while to think it over. And needless to say, my brothers should have equal say in it too."

"Fine. There's still time—though not much." His eyes roamed back to Chyenna. "And what about you, Ms. Dupres?"

Once again her glance flew to Blair's. This was the chance of a lifetime—not only for the Stagecoach Inn, but the entire town as well.

"My reply is the same as Mr. Westerman's—for now at least." Her stomach churned with apprehension. *A little while to think it over. In other words, time enough to think of a reason to say no?*

"I'm booked to fly back the thirtieth of this month, and I'll give you a call the minute I hit town. If you agree to the terms of the contract, we'll start shooting the following week."

"All right," Blair answered for both of them. "And just so there's no misunderstanding," he added, "I'm assuming this is an all-or-nothing deal, given your special circumstances and time constraints, of course."

"Correct." The scout righted his jaw, then continued. "Either you and Ms. Dupres come to a common agreement, or there's no agreement at all."

Sitting high in the saddle, Blair followed Lisa and Mandy as they wended their way alongside the creek. Yep, fall was definitely starting, he mused as he gazed about—no wonder the location scout had felt so pressed for time. Splashes of reds, greens, and gold were everywhere. And that morning, he noticed a new chill in the air.

Though George and Andy had intended to help trail cattle that afternoon, they'd soon discovered a yearling steer was about to be delivered, and had stayed back to attend to the birth.

The sun scorched Blair's back as they trotted along, picking their way through rocks and sage, stirring up columns of dust. Lisa was riding her favorite horse named Pegasus, while Mandy was atop Shadow—and already appearing very much at ease.

He was glad now the girls had been eager to take the lead. It gave him a chance to hang back a little and think things through, try to make some sense of it all.

Disturbing memories passed through his head: Chyenna's body pressed close to his, the floral scent of her freshly shampooed hair. Why had he allowed himself to kiss her?

Truth was, ever since that weekend back at Indianhead Springs, when he'd first met her, he'd longed to kiss her. Yet their physical contact that very morning had left him totally unprepared for the feelings that had soon followed. Confusion . . . desire . . . guilt . . . plus other emotions he couldn't quite put into words.

What happened—and thank God the girls had interrupted them—had made him confront himself in ways he'd never expected, never wanted, wasn't prepared to. Bottom line was, he was scared. Real scared.

He swallowed hard as his thoughts spun on, blending with the rhythm of the horse's clopping. He tightened his grip on the reigns. *Wise up, man, before you lose it altogether. Now's not the time to get yourself messed up with a woman . . . not if you know what's good for you.*

He glanced down at the parched, cracked earth. So far, no errant cattle, though he had spied a couple of rattlers and plenty of coyote sign. The cows always seemed to plant themselves on the creek bottom in hot weather, but maybe today he'd get lucky. He didn't have extra time this afternoon to load them into pickups and haul them back up to Mule Deer. And God only knew, George and Andy already had their hands full. . . .

"Oh, Daddy! Look!" Lisa called over her shoulder. The girls had stopped in their tracks and were pointing skyward. "The geese are flying south!"

Blair reined in his horse, and tipped back his head. He smiled. "I see them, darlin'! Seems they're startin' a little early this year."

"Cool!" Mandy shrieked. "Look how they fly in a big arrow! And it sounds like they're laughing!"

Blair couldn't help chuckling. "That's right, Mandy. Nothing quiet about migrating geese . . ."

For a split second, he wished Chyenna were here, too, sharing this moment, just like Martha sometimes had. Martha had never been much of a horsewoman, but she had agreed to help out once in a while. He'd cherished those times, hoped they'd grow into something larger, something they could share more often.

That, of course, had never come to fruition. Yet though the realization still hurt, somehow for the first time, it didn't cut quite so deeply.

They continued on, riding in silence. Chyenna, on the other hand, could never understand him, no matter how hard she tried. She could never appreciate his stewardship to the land, his struggle to survive—no more than Martha had. It was too much to expect from any woman who was born and raised in the city, no matter how strongly she might argue that she could change. Women like that were only kidding themselves.

Besides, he reminded himself, he and Chyenna had some serious business to hammer out. Chyenna undoubtedly considered Harry Clancer the proverbial goose who'd just laid at her feet the golden egg. It was a wonder she hadn't insisted they sign on the dotted line immediately, but for some reason she hadn't, thank God. Probably only because she realized he needed to first talk with George and Andy, which he planned to do over supper that night.

He lifted his gaze to the reddish brown buttes, like mammoth clay carvings against a never-ending horizon. Big land. Big sky. And a great big love for it all from deep inside his gut.

He felt his throat thicken with unspoken emotion.

Yep, he'd rather give up his very life than allow those city folk to ruin his land with their fancy RVs and movie sets, tromp down the native grasses, wildflowers, spook his cattle, plus all the other critters that shared squatting rights.

But most of all, he had his little daughter to consider. It was his job to protect Lisa. Shield her. Keep her from all those no-goods—not to mention the bad influence they'd wield. Oh yeah, he knew those Hollywood types . . .

That's what it all boiled down to in the end, didn't it? Looking out for Lisa? Keeping her out of harm's way? After all, that's why he hadn't wasted a moment high-tailing it back from L.A. after Martha had died. Yep, he had come home where he and Lisa belonged. Would always belong. And now Odyssey Productions could do the same damn thing.

Go back to L.A., where *they* belonged. . . .

They parked the pickup in the graveled lot of the pine-studded county park shortly after sunset. The darkening sky was streaked in shades of mauve, gray, and sherbet, yet despite the beauty that encompassed them, Chyenna couldn't shake off a strange, foreboding feeling. She and Blair were about to quarrel again, and she didn't want that. No, not for a minute.

Back at the ranch house that afternoon, they'd parted in silence, as if they both sensed they needed to be alone, not only to consider the scout's offer, but to recover from the emotional havoc their kisses had wrought. But now they were together again, driving high into the hills, knowing that sooner or later, they had no choice but to talk.

Inhaling deeply now, Chyenna peered straight ahead. The only living creature in sight was a gray digger squirrel which was sitting alert on an equally gray rock. The smell of sage drifted through the opened truck windows. In the waning daylight, the desert, the distant hills shimmered in muted earth tones tinged with violet.

"So what have you decided about Odyssey Productions?" she finally asked, breaking the strained silence as she met his piercing gaze.

He inclined his head—an endearing gesture that normally fascinated her, but right now the tension was too thick, too oppressive. At last he answered. "It's not good. As far as I'm concerned, the answer is no."

A sigh escaped her lips. "Now why doesn't that surprise me?"

"I suppose that means you disagree?"

"Absolutely. I think we ought to tell Harry whatever-his-name-is we'll go through with it."

"Harry *Clancer.*"

"All right." She gritted her teeth. "Harry Clancer." She turned and looked at Blair, tried again to ignore his eyes that seemed to dip into her very soul.

"Don't you see, Blair? This'll be a win-win situation on all sides. How can you even consider turning down an opportunity like this?"

He pulled his gaze away. "You already know how I feel about the summertime tourists. But that's not the half of it. What about every fall when the hunters flood in, trespass on our property, damage our fences? And if that's not bad enough, now some big hotshot studio from L.A., of all places, wants to move in on us too. You call *that* a win-win proposition?"

"Yes!" She felt the heat of frustration coloring her face. "The movie will not only put Prairie Valley on the map, it'll help my business and increase your profits too."

"Yeah, right."

"Excuse me? Are you trying to say you don't care about our financial futures?" she asked, her voice rising.

"The scout's offer was a come-on, Chyenna. A hook to grab our interest, draw us into his trap." Blair's voice hardened. "Why, I bet the bucks they're actually willing to fork over won't be anywhere near what he said."

"Maybe so. But don't forget, we're the ones holding the goods, Blair. At least we can use that to our advantage if, in the end, we should have to negotiate. As for me, I have no choice but to trust the scout. I have a daughter to support. It's up to me, and me alone."

"And so do I." Blair's eyes turned from mere cold to flinty blue ice. "But some things I just won't do. Even for money."

She pinched the bridge of her nose with her forefinger and thumb, trying to relieve the building tension. It wasn't working.

"I'm growing to love this valley as much as you do, Blair. Believe me. I want to stay. When my option to buy the inn comes due in another six weeks, I want to be solvent enough to do it. Then, too, there's Prairie Valley to consider. But unless we do something to keep our town from literally withering on the vine, we're going to lose it in other ways. Crucial ways. Sometimes sacrifices are unavoidable."

"It's not a matter of who sacrifices what," he insisted. "It's a matter of principle."

"The location shoot and support services will only be temporary," she reminded him. "I'll manage putting up with the inconveniences, as I'm sure you will too."

"Don't be too sure about that." His voice dropped. "And what about the girls? Have you stopped to consider how this might affect them?"

"What do you mean?"

"What I mean is, what if the movie shoot draws in some . . . how can I put it . . . some undesirable folks. God only knows what that might do to our little girls."

"Oh, Blair! That's ridiculous. Just think about the educational possibilities for them, the opportunity for personal growth. And when it comes to providing support services to the production crew, I'm sure they'd love to help. I mean, when they find out they have the chance to be meeting Billy Halligan and Bethany Daniels face-to-face, they're going to be frantic with excitement!"

"Darn it, Chyenna." He clenched his fist around the

steering wheel. "First you tell me I'm too hard on Lisa, that I need to give in and let her have a kitten. Now you're talking movie stars. That's an awful big jump, isn't it?"

"This is useless!" She threw up her hands in exasperation. "This is getting us absolutely nowhere. Take me home. Please."

"Yes, ma'am. Avoiding her eyes, he turned the key in the ignition with a little more gusto than necessary, then slammed the gears into reverse. "We're going. Right now."

Chapter Eight

Chyenna sat woodenly at the dining room table, staring into the dimly lit kitchen. She glanced up at the wall clock next to her china hutch. Two A.M. The clock's ticking filled the silent room, serving as a harsh reminder that time was slipping away on a personal level as well. What was she going to do? Before long, her lease would be up, and she'd be forced into deciding whether to purchase the inn or move on . . . where to, she didn't have a clue.

She wasn't ready to make that decision, that financial commitment. But ready or not, she'd be forced to do so soon. Too soon.

Leaning back, she closed her eyes. Granted, she was slowly gaining acceptance in the community, she reasoned, and next summer, her business would undoubtedly grow more. But for now, it was still touch and go. Given her large overhead, she was still barely breaking even. The added income from Odyssey Productions could make the crucial difference whether she stay or leave.

And now, she knew beyond the shadow of a doubt, she longed to stay. *Needed* to stay. Stay where not only her head, but ultimately her heart had led her.

The pitter-patter of feline feet sliced through her musing, and before she realized it, Ebony had chirped in catlike fashion and leaped into her lap. "You want to stay here, too, don't you, Ebony?" Chyenna murmured, stroking the cat's sleek, thick fur. "You like being a country cat that can hunt for mice and pounce on grasshoppers instead of being cooped up all day in a townhouse."

As if in answer, the cat chirped again, then immediately began purring.

Yet now there was Blair, Chyenna silently reminded herself, and his presence was threatening the very equanimity she so desperately yearned for. She could still feel his heat, his touch, his need, his own powerful awareness of her as a woman. To him their kisses had been nothing more than overactive hormones, though her own emotions had soared to greater heights, far beyond the mere physical. Indeed, it was almost as if she was falling in love with him—which she definitely was not. If their quarrel had proved anything to her, it should've been the stark reality of how ill-suited they were. She'd known that the first day they'd met, and she most definitely knew it now.

With a quick shake of her head she got to her feet. At five sharp the alarm would go off, and if she didn't get some sleep, she'd pay for it. Another full day loomed ahead: the monthly inventory, payroll, plus placing the food order for Blair's mother's reception, not to mention all the usual challenges of the regular work routine.

Still holding the cat, she tiptoed down the hallway and paused at Lisa's partially opened door. Struggling, Ebony jumped down and made a beeline for the foot of the bed, where, Chyenna decided, she'd most likely come from in the first place.

Moving inside the room, Chyenna gazed at her sleeping daughter and smiled. She was turned on one side, clutching her favorite teddy bear—though by the full light of day, Mandy would insist she was much too old for stuffed toys, especially now that she was back at school and already languishing over all the "cute" boys there. That, she decided with a wan smile, had undoubtedly stemmed from her friendship with Lisa.

As Chyenna continued to stare down at her, her heart ached with new love. *Ah, my little angel, she thought. My precious angel.* Her daughter looked so lovely, so serene, the corners of her mouth turned up in a slight smile as if she was dreaming only the most pleasant dreams.

Yes, dream on, my sweet one. Stay a child for as long as you can . . .

As Chyenna shut the door and strode back down the hallway, her thoughts returned to Blair. No, she couldn't allow herself to fall in love with him. Not if her life depended on it.

Fact of the matter was, she could never love any man, risk the chance of heartache for Mandy again. Never. Her daughter's rapidly fleeting childhood was too precious, and Mandy, herself, too vulnerable. She didn't need any more havoc in her young life, another father who would eventually flee. And even if she *were* to fall in love with Blair, he could never love her in return. He was too guilt ridden. Still imprisoned by his personal demons.

Yes, she and Lisa had no choice but to make it on their own. And God help them, they would, she promised herself. They'd keep striving toward that goal, find new meaning, new peace.

But when Chyenna had finally dragged herself into her own bed and tried in vain to sleep, her thoughts were anything but peaceful.

Blair sat hunched over, grinding the lens for his newest telescope, trying at the same time not to grind his teeth in frustration.

All night so far, sleep had eluded him, so he figured he might as well try to catch up on some work in his shop. But that wasn't going so well either. Try as he did, he just couldn't seem to concentrate.

He removed the telescope mirror, preparing to clean it in a solution of distilled water and mild soap. But as he carried the mirror over to the utility sink, his thoughts kept bouncing back to his quarrel with Chyenna. He'd been thinking about that all evening, and the more he did, the more upset he got. No matter how diplomatic he'd tried to be, she'd been totally unreasonable.

He stopped working long enough to rub the ache at the back of his neck. Sometimes he wished he'd never met Chyenna Dupres. In fact, life would definitely be much simpler if she'd never moved here—though he was still convinced she wouldn't be sticking around much longer, at least not beyond the time her lease was up.

But their differences about the location shoot were just the tip of the iceberg. Perhaps the real reason he'd lashed out was because the feelings she'd stirred inside him were downright unnerving. Why, it'd only been a little over six weeks since he'd first met her, and now he never wanted to let her go. Ever. It was almost as if their destiny had been written in the stars, and they were both at a complete loss to do anything about it.

Ridiculous! He lunged to his feet. There was no such thing as destiny, not romantically speaking, at least. Even he and Martha had been completely mismatched, and as much as he had loved her and grieved for her, if she hadn't died, she would have probably eventually left him anyway. What made him think it'd be any different with Chyenna?

He shook his head. Nope, the idea of star-crossed lovers was right out of some fairy tale, folklore, a yarn like Chyenna would undoubtedly spin—or worse, encourage the girls to do.

You're losing it, man. Going totally whacko. Better get some sleep before you talk yourself into any more stupidity.

He locked up the shop and strode back through the night shadows to the ranch house, with only the sound of the hoot owls and the howl of the coyotes mingling with his thoughts. Angling his gaze across the field, he spied the inn. A dim light illuminated the upstairs window that faced his property, a light that he'd never noticed before. Was Chyenna, by any chance, having problems sleeping too? Thinking about their fiery kisses in the hayloft, their words of anger later that evening?

Yep, they'd quarreled all right. And he might as well forget about going over there to try to patch things up. Because he knew, sure as shootin', it wouldn't do one bit of good. They were simply from two different worlds, and it was hopeless to think they'd ever agree.

A short time later with a pad and pencil in hand, he settled down at the kitchen table, and beneath a pool of light from the gooseneck lamp, started writing. Cowboy poetry. He'd made at least a dozen attempts at it, so far, and each time he had, it seemed easier to express his feelings.

A cowboy's life is hard work and sweat,
Riding and roping and staying out of debt,
But when the stars and moon come out at night
Sending down their heavenly light,
Then his thoughts turn to good times—both big and
*   small,*
And courting the women, some short, some tall,
But let me tell you, partner, there's trouble in store,
When the cowboy kisses his woman—and that's for
*   shore,*
'Cause a cowgirl with true grit is mighty hard to find,
Especially one who's the marrying kind,
So listen up, each and every buckaroo,
And heed my advice if you're wondering what to do,
The kisses and good times, that might be all right,
But stay away from women when the stars come out at
*   night.*

"Mama! Mama! The people are coming!" Mandy pulled back the curtain and peered through the kitchen window. "Hurry, Mama! We've still got to put the ice ring in the punch bowl! And oh, one more thing—I'm supposed to help Lisa pass out the groom's cake!"

"Don't worry. Everything's nearly done." Chyenna followed her daughter's gaze onto the parking lot that fronted the grange hall. Several dozen guests had gathered on the front lawn, laughing and chatting, while more cars continued to pull in.

"What's everybody doing? Why are they just standing around that way?"

"They're probably waiting for the bride and groom." Chyenna rinsed her hands, then dried them on a terry cloth towel.

"I gotta go, now, Mama! Lisa said I should meet her by the front door."

"Have fun."

Quick as a flash, Mandy shrugged out of her white pinafore apron, slung it over a coat rack by the door and scampered outside, red French braids flying. As Chyenna watched her leave, she couldn't help but smile to herself. All week long, both Mandy and Lisa had been so thrilled about the upcoming wedding, they'd barely discussed anything else.

"When *I* get married," she'd overheard Mandy announce to Lisa, "I want you to promise to be my maid of honor." Lisa, of course, had not only agreed, but made Mandy promise she'd reciprocate.

Pulling her attention back to her work, Chyenna finished garnishing the potato salad with a few sprigs of parsley. *What a perfect day for a wedding,* she thought. It was the last weekend in September, a gorgeous Indian summer day, painted in splashes of gold and blue. Right now sunlight was streaming through the kitchen window—that pale, muted sunlight so typical of autumn. In the sprawling field across from the grange hall, pumpkins ripened, looking like giant golden coins. The faint hint of wood smoke hung in the air.

Chyenna's mind drifted back to another wedding, another time. Ten years ago . . . ten years ago on a Saturday afternoon, sunny and warm a lot like today. She could almost still smell the heady scent of the roses in her bridal bouquet, feel Dan's large hand, warm and protective around hers, and hear him whisper, "My darling, you're finally mine. Forever."

Forever. She gave a quick shake of her head, sighing. Forever had been nothing more than nine bittersweet years. What had happened? she wondered now as she had a thousand times before. Hadn't her love for Dan been enough?

"Chyenna?" The speaker was Rosita Gonzales, one of the on-call employees who'd agreed to help today.

"Uh . . . yes?" Chyenna looked up with a start and forced a wobbly smile.

"Are you feeling all right?" Rosita asked. "I noticed a cot in the back room. Maybe you should go lie down."

Chyenna smiled again and tried to sound nonchalant. "Thanks for your concern, Rosie, but I'm really quite fine."

Nan, who was cutting melon balls for the fruit salad and just happened to be eavesdropping, chimed in. "I suspect what's bothering Chyenna right now is the same thing that's bothering me."

"Oh? What's that?" Rosie asked.

Nan pulled a face. "Chicken fat! I swear, if I never

have to skin another chicken again, that'll suit me just fine."

The three women chuckled, nodding in agreement.

"Next event we cater, I'll make sure my supplier gets it right," Chyenna told them. "No more unskinned chicken!"

They chuckled again. No one, however, mentioned the other mishaps that had occurred so far: Mandy dropping several champagne glasses and breaking them, Chyenna having to run back into town to purchase more cocktail ice and cut flowers, plus the horror they'd all experienced about an hour earlier when the hot dishes were in the oven, and a brief thunderstorm had caused the electricity to fail.

Heading into the adjoining dining hall, Chyenna popped the ice ring from its mold and placed it into the punch bowl, then glanced about. The buffet table looked lovely. Candlelight glimmered from the candelabra. Platters were heaped with juicy barbecued ribs, chicken cordon bleu, corn on the cob, yeast rolls, an array of salads, and vegetarian entrees. At the far end stood the most elegant tiered wedding cake Chyenna had ever seen.

The room, as well, appeared festive and romantic, just as Blair's mother had hoped. Candle votives sparkled from the center of round tables draped in pale pink linen. Garlands of silk flowers, interspersed with ivy, hung from the doorways and above the windows.

Footsteps sounded in the foyer, then a burst of talking and laughter. "Oh good!" Nan said, coming alongside Chyenna. "The party's finally ready to begin!"

"Yes, and just look at the bride and groom!" Chyenna couldn't help the small thrill that flared inside her. "Don't they look absolutely radiant?"

"*More* than radiant!" Nan enthused, smiling.

Sharon, pretty and petite in a pastel blue linen suit, was nodding to several people in the room and smiling. The groom, a short stocky man with a balding head and lopsided grin, stopped several times to shake hands with the guests. Lisa and Mandy trailed behind, grinning like Cheshire cats as they passed out small packets of groom's cake in gold foil and blue ribbons.

"Oh, wow," Nan said, looking farther beyond. "And guess who's next? Blair Westerman. Isn't he a sight to behold?" She crossed her arms over her chest and sent Chyenna a knowing look. "And if I were you, girl, I'd get an eyeful, because you ain't gonna see him dressed up like this very often."

When isn't he a sight to behold? Chyenna almost blurted out, but already Nan had started back to the kitchen. Nan was right. Blair did look stunning— though slightly uncomfortable—in a black tux with a starched white shirt and wide burgundy cumberbund. Next to him were two other men also decked out in their formal best, undoubtedly his brothers, though she still wasn't certain which one was George, and which one was Andy. An attractive young blond was close by the taller man's side, and it was obvious they, too, were deeply in love.

Chyenna turned on her heel and started for the kitchen, but not without first stealing one more look at Blair. A couple of women had just cornered him—one with black shoulder-length hair and heavy makeup, the other a coy-looking redhead. The women were flirting openly and Blair seemed to be enjoying every minute of it.

Chyenna sighed. She was jealous, plain and simple. Jealous of any woman who dared even look twice at him. Yet she and Blair had barely spoken together these past two weeks, she kept reminding herself. What gave her the right to think she had any holds on him?

Soon the party was in full swing. Somehow Chyenna managed to keep her thoughts focused on her work as she kept the platters piled high while the other women bussed tables. But when it came time for Blair to propose a toast to the bride and groom, she could no longer deny to herself how much she'd missed him. Missed his smile, the teasing sparkle in his blue eyes, his laughter. Why did he possess such a hold on her? she wondered miserably. She and Mandy didn't need another man. Ever. Especially one who was so wrong for her in every way.

A hush fell over the room as Blair tugged self-consciously at his black tie, then began to speak.

"Friends, family . . . first, on behalf of the families

of the bride and groom, I'd like to thank each and everyone of you for helping share this most happy day. We realize that our mother and Rusty are starting a new chapter in their lives and I'm sure I can speak for everyone here when I say we wish them well, a wonderful future, and continued love."

Blair paused, dropped his gaze for a fleeting second, then lifted it again to Sharon, whose eyes were shimmering with tears of happiness. "And as for you, Ma, your sons are so proud of you, we're almost bustin' the fancy buttons off these blasted starched shirts we were forced to wear." A ripple of laughter skittered about the room. "Seriously though," Blair continued, "your family would like to thank you for all your love, support, and guidance, especially these last few years when the goin' got tough. We know it hasn't always been easy for you . . . but . . . but we've admired you for your courage and inspiration." Blair lifted his champagne glass. "And now I propose a toast to you and your terrific husband. May you both always reap one hundredfold the happiness you've given to others."

"Here, here." The guests murmured their agreement and lifted their champagne glasses. The sound of clinking could be heard from every corner of the room.

Oh, Blair, Chyenna thought with a lump in her throat. *Stop for a moment to look and listen. Look at your mother. Listen to what you've just said. If she can put her past behind her and start over again, why can't you?*

"And now ladies and gents!" The D.J.'s exclamation sliced through Chyenna's thoughts. "It's time for the bride and groom to lead off the first dance!"

In no time, Rusty was spinning Sharon around the room to a countrified rendition of "Hawaiian Wedding Song." Soon others joined in till a sea of bobbing heads filled the dance floor. One dance gave way to another and another, from slow twangy waltzes to high-stepping line dances.

Looking on, Chyenna rested her weight against the frame of the kitchen door, an empty serving tray in one hand. She smiled to herself. Grandparents danced with grandchildren. Sisters danced with brothers. Sweethearts, young and old, swayed arm-in-arm. There was so much joy, so much love here, she could almost reach out and touch it. What a difference from the phony social gatherings she'd attended in the city, she thought, where the cocktail parties and so-called charity events were often driven by anything but love.

"Wake up, Miss Dreamy-eyes. May I have this dance?"

Blair! Her stomach took a giant nosedive.

"Sorry, Westerman," she replied more crisply than she'd intended. "I got clean-up to do."

The look in his eyes told her he didn't buy it. "Chyenna." He paused for emphasis. "You gonna dance with me or not?"

"Not." She promptly turned, and, gripping the tray harder than necessary, started to walk away.

He promptly took the tray from her, set it down on a table, and pulled her into his arms. The strains of an old Roy Orbison song filled the room.

"That's more like it," he murmured into her ear, pulling her close.

She tried to resist, but couldn't. She'd longed for him too much. Had hungered for his touch a thousand times over. And now . . . now the feeling of his lean, muscled body pressed close, the intoxicating sound of his voice. She was losing the battle. She was powerless to fight it. Desperately playing her last card, she said, "This isn't in my job description. I'm supposed to be working, not dancing."

"Ah, and they say *I'm* a workaholic," he muttered.

She felt her mouth go dry. Just this one dance, she promised herself. One dance only, and no more.

"You've been avoiding me." His voice was husky, low. She felt his warm breath fanning her ear.

"No more than you've been avoiding me."

"Okay. We'll call it even." He grazed his hand down her back, leaving a scorching trail. "But the real issue is our unfinished business . . ."

"How could I forget?" She pulled back, trying to quiet her escalating emotions. "Please, Blair, let's not discuss it now." *I want to dance with you, hold you, foolishly pretend you're mine, just for a few more precious moments.*

"Fair enough." He narrowed his gaze, thinking. "Tell

you what. I'll stick around till after the party's over. Help clean up . . . whatever. Then when everyone's gone, we'll talk."

"All right." She gave an indifferent shrug, but her insides were quaking. Would this turn into a replay of their earlier disagreement? Would she end up saying things she might regret later? She couldn't bear more verbal sparring. No, not on this day filled with such happiness and new beginnings . . .

They continued dancing in silence as one tune led to another, and though she realized she'd already dismissed her silent one-dance limit, she also realized she wanted it this way. Pressed together, swaying to the music. Her head against his chest, feeling his warmth, immersing herself in his awesome male power . . .

Yes, Blair's nearness left her totally disarmed. Visions of their kisses in the hayloft shimmered through her mind. *This is a mistake, a humongous mistake,* she chided herself. And all the while she was sinking deeper and deeper, at a loss to stop herself.

"Chyenna?" Blair planted a gentle kiss on the top of her head, causing fresh waves of wanting to crash over her.

"Hmm?"

"Can we bury the ax for a while? Long enough, at least, to get back to being civil to each other—especially since we still need to talk?"

"I'd like that too." She exhaled slowly. True enough,

they might never see eye-to-eye about the movie filming, but it would be nice to be back on friendly terms again.

She felt him tense as he continued. "Uh . . . there's something else."

"Oh?" She drew back a fraction.

"I realize now that I've been blinded to some of my daughter's needs . . . but . . . but Lisa and I are working it out. I'm happy to say we're doing much better."

"Oh, Blair." She closed her eyes, rested her head on his shoulder. "I'm so glad to hear that. And I'm sorry too. I was just as much at fault for quarreling."

She smiled up at him. In an instant, his mouth sought hers. Softly at first, like the touch of a butterfly's wings. She linked both arms around his neck, welcoming him. His lips lingered, and though he kept the kiss chaste, she could taste his hunger, his need.

When they'd finished kissing, Chyenna glanced over her shoulder and caught sight of the two women who'd been flirting with Blair. They were staring, open-mouthed, practically throwing daggers at her with their eyes. "If looks could kill," she whispered to Blair, "you and I'd already be six feet under."

"What?"

"Those women." She jerked her head in their direction. "I assume you're acquainted?"

He looked over. "Oh, them," he said dryly. "That's just Lucy Pinkerton and her cousin, Amber. I sometimes shoot pool with them at Duffy's Grill." Amusement threaded his voice as he added, "I'll introduce you if you like, when we're done dancing."

"Thanks, but no thanks. Besides, I'm getting the impression one of them might be planning to cut in on us any moment now."

"Just let them try," he growled, pulling her closer. "Tonight I'm dancing with nobody but you."

Chapter Nine

Blair flung the mop back and forth across the grange hall floor, mulling things over. While Chyenna and Nan had loaded the last food supplies into cardboard crates and transported them outside to their cars, he'd changed into the T-shirt and jeans he'd brought with him.

Everyone had left, even the girls who'd gone back to the ranch house with George and his fiancée, Sarah. Earlier they'd rented a movie to watch on the VCR, and George had promised they'd pop corn and drink fresh apple cider.

All evening Blair had been sweating it, thinking about the moment he'd have no choice but to introduce Chyenna to his brothers. And that moment had come with as much awkwardness as he'd anticipated. George, of course, hadn't missed a beat showing his interest, his thinly veiled hope that Blair's association with Chyenna might lead to something more . . .

Andy, though a bit bashful at first, had warmed to Chyenna immediately. Blair was willing to bet his bottom dollar he'd get plenty of razzing from Andy later when they were alone—especially about the way he and Chyenna had kissed right there in the middle of the dance floor. "Before long that little gal will have you eatin' right out of her hand," Blair could almost hear Andy say. "You were always a sucker for a pretty woman, big brother, and this one's no exception."

Then, of course, there was Ma—Ma and Rusty heading out the door this very moment, eager to get off on their honeymoon on the Oregon coast. He'd certainly meant every word when he'd proposed the toast and wished them the best. But had Ma needed to keep harping so much these last few weeks, saying what a wonderful wife Chyenna would make some lucky man?

He carried the bucket through a side door and heaved the dirty water into an empty planter box as his thoughts rolled on. Well, he had news for Ma—and anyone else who might have such fool notions. That lucky man could never be him. Oh, it wasn't that Chyenna wasn't one sexy, classy lady. She was. Just the very sight of her tonight had made him get hot under the collar. But what Chyenna deserved was a husband, a soul mate for the long haul, not a one-night stand. She deserved a man who would take care of her, give her the world, not a floundering cattle rancher who was nearly drowning in a mountain of debt.

"I've been doing some hard thinking," Blair said without preamble. It was shortly after midnight, and he and Chyenna were sitting outside on Adirondack chairs on the screen-covered porch. His pickup and her van were the only two vehicles remaining in the grange lot, parked at opposite ends.

"Ah, a deep thinker. That's what I like." She darted him a playful look, then sobered. "Sorry, Blair. I couldn't resist. But seriously, what's on your mind?"

He appeared unfazed by her teasing remark. "I think we *should* sign the contract with the movie company. I'm assuming you're still interested too?" he added after a moment's hesitation.

"Are you kidding?" she exclaimed, nearly jumping for joy. "I'm more than interested! I'm thrilled."

The air smelled sweet with the scent of a brief rain shower, but even sweeter, it seemed, now that Blair had told her what she'd been dying to hear. Crickets chirped from the field across the road. To the west, the clouds had parted and a crescent moon hung against the purple night sky like a giant comma.

She hesitated, then found the courage to ask. "But what made you suddenly change your mind?"

"I talked it over with my brothers. We decided that since the location shoot shouldn't last much longer than a week, we can put up with the hassle." Grim determination laced his voice as he added, "But we need to hold Clancer to every penny of his offer, Chyenna. That's the only way this crazy ordeal will be worth it to us. Any of us."

"Yes, of course. That's exactly how I feel too."

"I want this to be as clean as possible. If Clancer tries to back down from his original price, the deal's off."

She nodded. How typical of Blair to want it this way. Straightforward and simple. No strings attached. "But we'll need to be very careful," she pointed out. "We can't afford to lose this opportunity."

"I realize that. And I'm convinced we won't, not if we play our cards right." Blair heaved a sigh. "Heck! For all we know, Clancer might not show up at all! Maybe by now he's found a better spot."

"I doubt it. He seemed dead set on doing the shoot right here. And he did say there wasn't much time for checking out other options."

"True enough, I suppose. But are you sure you're still willing to feed the entire crew . . . the support services, or whatever fancy name he called it? The way Clancer talked, the numbers could mount up fast."

"Yes. I can do it. After tonight, I've proved that to myself." She hesitated. "What were George and Andy's reactions when you told them about Clancer?"

"George was as cautious as I was, but after we kicked it around for a while, he agreed to go for it. After all, he's got his fiancée, Sarah, to consider now too." One corner of Blair's mouth lifted in a half smile. "And

Andy? Well, who knows about Andy? One minute he can be one hundred percent for something, and the next minute, dead set against it. But in the end, he usually defers most of the business decisions to George and me. All our little brother really cares about is doing the rodeo circuits, ropin' cattle, and courtin' good-looking women."

Chyenna stared at the headlights of a distant car as it wound its way down a dark hillside, all the while fully cognizant of Blair's eyes on her.

"We have our squabbles, like any family," he continued. "But somehow we do manage to make it all work." He slipped his arm over her shoulder, but his touch felt awkward, restrained. "And as far as George and Sarah go . . . well, they're still all caught up making cow eyes at each other. Just give them three or four years of marriage, and then they'll see what life's really all about."

"Gosh, Blair!" She gave a humorless laugh. "And I thought *I* was jaded when it comes to marriage."

"We aren't jaded, Chyenna, just realistic. We've learned from past experience."

"But I thought you and Martha were happy, very much in love."

"We were." He shook his head. "But sometimes love just isn't enough."

"Meaning?" This was the first time she'd heard Blair voice doubts about his marriage, and the sudden revelation left her a trifle shaken.

"I hated living in the big city as much as Martha

hated living in the country. "Oh, don't get me wrong. I did enjoy working at L.A. Scientific. My job was to test the telescopes before shipping each order out. But at the same time, I felt hemmed in, roped to my desk, while all the time what I really wanted was to be back in the wide open spaces, roping cattle instead." He stopped, stared off into the darkness, then continued in a low voice. "It wasn't long till Martha and I'd started bickering more and more . . . about little things . . . petty things . . . things that, looking back now, didn't really matter that much. She knew I was unhappy, but of course, she'd been unhappy too." He shrugged. "And . . . and even if Martha hadn't died, I'm not too sure our marriage would've survived anyway."

They fell silent, each struggling to deny the spiraling tension, like an ominous dark shadow.

It's almost as if Martha's sitting here between us, watching, listening, Chyenna cautioned herself. Earlier that evening when Chyenna and Blair had kissed on the dance floor, she'd anticipated this time together alone. But it seemed now, *alone* was an impossibility.

I can't do this. I can't let this go on. No matter what he says now about their marriage, he did love her. He loves her still. His guilt and doubts have just muddied the waters. She dug her fingernails into her palms and stared unseeingly across the shadowy front yard. The lacy foliage of the weeping willow stirred slightly in the breeze.

"Tell me about your mother's wedding," she said, diverting the conversation. "I would've loved to have been there."

He shifted his weight. "Well, I guess you'd call it a typical country wedding in a typical country church. Small town pastor and plenty of people filling the pews. When all was said and done, it was over in about half an hour."

"In other words, short and to the point."

"Right." His brow furrowed. "Actually, I hadn't set foot in that church since Martha was around—that is, till today, of course."

Martha again. How is it he keeps coming back to Martha? Well, at least he's talking about her now, that's good. But somehow, now that he is, Martha's presence seems more looming than ever.

"You were married there too?" she asked evenly.

"Yep, but that's only the half of it. Her funeral was also in that church. I had her body flown from L.A.," he added, his voice choked. He cleared his throat. "Since most of her family was gone, and the majority of mine lived right here, it made the most sense."

She reached out to squeeze his hand, "Oh, Blair. I'm sorry." Ambivalence gnawed inside her. In light of the anguish he was trying so hard to hide, her own turmoil now seemed trivial and selfish. Still, selfish or not, her feelings were undeniably real and try as she did, she couldn't just push them aside.

"Looking back," he went on, "I probably shouldn't

have avoided the church as long as I did. Sort of like fallin' off a horse and gettin' back on, you know?" He squared his jaw, righted it again, then continued raggedly. "I'm sorry, Chyenna. I . . . I didn't mean to ramble on this way."

"Don't apologize. This . . . this is a good thing."

He stood up. A weary smile washed across his face. "Well, time to call it a night, I guess."

"Yes . . . yes, it *is* getting late."

She got to her feet also, keeping a safe distance away. How she longed to hold him tight, kiss him as he'd never been kissed before . . . but it was too late now. It could never be, for the magic had shattered and vanished into thin air.

The first week of October swept in like a flamboyant leading lady. Indian summer gilded the hills in crimson, burnt orange and buff, lending a resplendent contrast to the blue skies. White puffs of clouds scudded by while more geese flew in V-formation, trumpeting loudly.

Meanwhile, the Stagecoach Inn and the Triple Y Ranch were bursting with activity. The location scout's follow-up trip to Prairie Valley resulted in a quick execution of the contract. Chyenna and Blair had received their full negotiated price.

Now directors, makeup artists, and sound technicians were dashing in every direction. At the inn, the sign that fronted the parking lot said *The Rustlers' Inn* in bold, rustic letters. And down the road, the Triple Y sign had been changed to the *Whistling Willows Ranch.*

Meanwhile, every day that week, throngs of people gathered on the set to watch. News about the location shoot—for it had made headlines in all the local newspapers—drew long distance travelers and day trippers alike.

"Yesterday when I gassed up at the Jack Pot station," Nan told Chyenna as they were slicing roast beef through a commercial food processor, "Harry Mosier had some encouraging news."

Chyenna grinned, holding up one hand. "Wait! Let me guess. I bet he told you he's pumping so much gas he can hardly keep up with it all."

"Right. How did you know?"

"Because that's exactly what he told me too," Chyenna answered with a laugh.

"And that's not all," Nan put in. "I also heard that at the Shop & Save, the sale of take-out food and beverages has almost tripled."

Chyenna twisted the lid shut on the mustard jar, then reached for a sandwich bag. "I sure hope Blair's sitting up and taking notice."

The women exchanged knowing grins, then fell silent as they continued working. These past several days, they too, were outdoing themselves. They'd dished up more hamburgers, hot dogs, sandwiches, and fried chicken than they'd ever dreamed possible. And though the inn was closed to the general public during the film shoot, no one needed to tell them that when they opened again, business would be booming.

Meanwhile, Blair kept a watchful eye, remaining covertly inconspicuous. The few times Chyenna had asked him to run into town for more supplies, he'd been reserved, though cooperative. He'd also driven the girls to school each day and Thursday afternoon to their 4-H meeting.

As often as they could, Mandy and Lisa helped with the support services—that is, when they weren't busy posing as extras. Much to their delight, they'd been selected to participate in a crowd scene outside the inn where Billy Halligan and his men—in a whirlwind of dust, noise and action—gunned down a horse thief. The twenty-year-old actor, with his rock hard muscles and blond good looks was indeed the current teen heartthrob wherever he went. The two girls, especially Lisa, seemed his biggest fans.

"Isn't Billy Halligan the cutest guy ever!" Lisa enthused to Mandy one evening as they'd strolled back to the inn.

"He's more than cute!" Mandy agreed, sighing. "He's dreamy!" Carefully they picked their way through the trucks, trailers, and motorhomes where the actors and production staff had retired for the night. Some were parked in the lot at the inn, others, on Blair's property alongside the creek bank.

"And I still can't believe it!" Mandy went on. "We're gonna be in a real Hollywood movie! A movie with Billy Halligan! The kids at school are so jealous!"

"Oh, I'm *sooo* in love," Lisa said, holding a hand to her heart, then bursting into giggles.

"Me too." Mandy mimicked her friend's gesture.

"You're too young to fall in love," Lisa scoffed condescendingly. "People don't fall in love till they're at least almost twelve like me . . ."

"Who says I'm too young?"

"I do! Anybody knows nine is practically still a baby."

"Is not!"

"Is too!"

"Well, I know something that you don't know," Mandy taunted. She rolled her eyes and allowed a long dramatic pause to follow.

"What?"

"Today I overheard Mom telling Nan that Billy donated a ton of money to the city to fix the swimming pool and make it bigger and better. There'll even be money to build a movie theater." She rolled her eyes again before adding, "And guess what?"

"What?"

"They're even gonna name it after Billy!"

Too bad he couldn't stick around more to watch the film shoot, Blair thought as he maneuvered his three-wheeler up the rutted land to Mule Deer. Too bad for two reasons. Number one, he should be keeping an eye on the action, make sure no one was impacting his land any more than necessary. And number two, most important of all, he should be keeping a closer eye on Lisa. He hadn't missed that 100-watt smile on her face every time Billy Halligan walked by, nor the way she and Mandy had plotted to talk to him like some darn lovesick groupies. For all he knew, Chyenna had probably been making eyes at him too! The thought brought an alarming stab of jealousy.

But for now, the cattle had to be trucked back down before the snows started to fly. George and Andy were due to meet him at Mule Deer in a couple of hours to do exactly that.

He shifted gears as he rounded the next bend, kicking up a trail of dust. Scrub pine and sage whirred past him. *Thank God the film shoot will be done by tomorrow. The publicity is drawing too many gawkers, making it seem like summer all over again—only worse.* Why, just the other day in town, when he attempted to cross at 3rd and Main, the traffic was so steady, he thought he would never get through.

But aside from the crowds and hassles, he had to concede there was one bright spot. For the girls' sake, he was happy they'd been chosen to work as extras. Ever since Martha had died, he'd never seen Lisa so alive, so exhilarated. Chyenna would be quick to point out, too, that the experience would boost their confidence, stretch their horizons—and maybe she was right.

He slowed the three-wheeler as he came to a fork in

the road, then turned right. Gunning the engine, he zoomed up the pine-studded hillside where ribbons of mottled sunlight danced on the forest floor. He caught scent of the backwoods, the clean crisp air. Above through the treetops, a hawk soared.

Ah, yes, God's country, he thought with a smile as he had so many times in the past. The best place in the world to raise kids. And speaking of that, Lisa's birthday, and the pack trip he'd promised her, were only a couple of days away.

He crested the next hill, then dipped down again as the road narrowed, all the time mapping out a plan in his mind. Maybe he'd talk to Chyenna about helping him bake a surprise birthday cake for Lisa. The old log cabin, fueled by a generator, offered all the comforts of home. And hopefully Chyenna would agree, because if she didn't, he surely would be in a pickle! Truth was, he'd never baked a cake in his entire life.

But the best part—whether she agreed or not—was that he'd finally have Chyenna alone. Alone for a long, lazy weekend, tucked away in the hills. He gave a wry laugh, quickly amending his thoughts. As much alone as two people could be with their precocious little daughters in tow, that is.

He would have been a fool this past week not to have seen the leering come-ons and ogling looks certain male members of Odyssey Productions had cast Chyenna's way. And he was jealous, admittedly jealous! The jealousy had made his temperature rise, his blood boil, and he'd had all he could do to keep from taking those fools down. Chyenna, however, had merely laughed off their advances in that enticing little way of hers, making him want her all the more.

Yep, a weekend with Chyenna would be a welcomed treat. He swallowed hard. If only weekends could last forever . . .

Chapter Ten

By Friday evening peace and order once again reigned over Prairie Valley, especially at the ranch and the inn. Now Odyssey Productions and the location shoot were only a fading memory, but nevertheless, one that had left its impact on both the community and its inhabitants.

Chyenna basked in the knowledge that at last she was financially solvent. In only a matter of a few more weeks she'd be signing her next contract, the one that would give her ownership of the inn. The prospect left her lighthearted, practically soaring.

The Westerman brothers were also sleeping better at night. Now, regardless of falling cattle prices, they could pay off a sizable portion of their debts, and still reap a significant profit.

Prairie Valley, of course, would never be the same. Down at city hall, plans for the swimming pool renovation and new movie theater were already underway with the promise of increased revenue and new jobs. Meanwhile, clips of the movie shoot had appeared on news broadcasts throughout the Northwest, and a local novelty shop was silk screening T-shirts that read "Prairie Valley Goes to Hollywood."

Yet the greatest change of all had little to do with money and profits and civic enhancements. It was seeing Blair Westerman standing first in line with a big grin on his face when the shop first started taking orders. He'd promised the girls he'd buy one for each of them.

"This campout couldn't have come at a better time, even if it wasn't Lisa's birthday." Chyenna tossed another log onto the campfire, then rubbing her hands together briskly, plopped down on the red and black plaid wool blanket next to Blair. It was Saturday, not quite dusk, at Mule Deer.

After an early supper around the campfire of frankfurters, veggie dogs, baked beans and potato salad—for they were all indeed ravenous after the seven-mile trek—Lisa and Mandy had hurried back to the cabin to wash dishes, then frost the birthday cake. Double chocolate with fudge icing, Lisa had insisted excitedly. With Chyenna's help, Blair had mixed the flour, sugar, cocoa, and other ingredients that afternoon after they'd arrived, then he popped the batter into the small oven at the cabin. Soon the sunny kitchen was fairly bursting with the delicious aroma of the baking cake.

"Better time for you or the girls?" Blair asked.

"Actually, for all of us." She sent him a guarded smile. "Maybe—just maybe—it'll help bring our daughters back down to earth and forget about Billy Halligan."

The entire way up the trail that morning, they'd giggled and talked about no one other than the gorgeous young actor, even more a hero in their eyes now that he'd helped save their town.

"I'm gonna keep my autographed picture of him forever," Lisa had raved. "And I even brought it along in my backpack."

"Yeah, but what good is one stupid picture when we'll probably never even see him again in person." Mandy was still wallowing in her sadness over his leaving. "Oh gosh, it makes me want to cry every time I even think of it . . ."

Still, despite the constant chatter, the preadolescent angst, the pack trip to Mule Deer had not only been gorgeous, but rejuvenating. Chyenna quickly learned that Dancer and the two other llamas, a honey-colored gelding named Baja and a black female called Licorice, were very sure-footed on the rutted trails. Because Lisa and Mandy had already taken the llamas for shorter "practice" treks on the lower ranch, they were sufficiently trained in being haltered, saddled, and led.

Moreover, these peaceful, yet curious creatures had

seemed to enjoy the trek as much as the humans had. Each llama had carried about fifty pounds of food, clothing, and bedrolls, yet had caused less damage to the trail than the horses did. At present, they were grazing in the small corral not far from the cabin.

Blair looked up at the sky, felt the sharp east wind. "It's gonna get mighty cold out here tonight."

She smiled as he urged her closer and she snuggled into him. Yes, there was a definite frostiness in the air. But the woodsy scent of the campfire, the sighing of the wind in the treetops, and cuddling like this with Blair was nothing short of heaven on Earth.

"Camping in our tent last summer was certainly a new and wonderful experience," she told him. "But I have to agree, the promise of a soft cot, heat and hot water seems wonderful."

In the flickering glow of the firelight, his grin was enticing. "Hmm . . . you sound a lot like my ma. She always insists that her idea of camping is staying in a plush hotel with a chocolate left on her pillow and room service." His arm tightened around her.

She laughed and stared into the campfire as her heart beat out a triple tattoo. The fire popped and crackled. The embers glowed crimson, the flames curled around the blackened logs.

"Happy birthday to me! Happy birthday to me!" The sound of Lisa's singing, coupled by Mandy's laughter, sliced through their conversation.

Lisa emerged from the shadows carrying the just

frosted cake in a rectangular pan, candles flickering, but during the time it'd taken them to return, at least half of the candles had blown out. Mandy brought up the rear with paper plates, plastic forks, and luckily a book of matches.

Lisa set the cake on the makeshift table Blair had created from a couple of logs and a piece of plywood. Then she and Mandy sat down on the other side of the campfire on the foam pads they'd put there earlier.

"Oh no!" Mandy cried, smacking her palm over her mouth.

"What's wrong?" Lisa cried.

"I forgot the knife to cut the cake!"

"We'll use my pocketknife," Blair volunteered as he dug into his hip pocket.

"I hope it's clean," Lisa said warily.

"Of course it is, darlin'." He broke into a wide grin. "Matter of fact, I haven't used it since that last time I dished up a big old batch of Rocky Mountain oysters!"

"Oh, Daddy! That's so gross!"

"What's Rocky Mountain oysters?" Mandy piped up.

Blair's grin grew wider, but before he could answer Lisa had already shrieked, "You wanna know what Rocky Mountain oysters are? *I'll* tell you what they are!"

"What?" Chyenna and Mandy chorused.

"Calf testicles!"

Mandy burst into a fit of giggles while Chyenna felt her face turning hot.

"What's testicles?" Mandy whispered to Lisa.

"I'll tell you later," Lisa whispered back behind a cupped hand. "First, I think I'm gonna be sick."

Blair was obviously enjoying the stir he'd created.

"Hey, what's the big deal, ladies? Rocky Mountain oysters make mighty good grub. Yep, delicious! They taste even better than fried chicken!"

"That's what they say about every poor unlikely creature's body parts that end up in someone's frying pan," Chyenna muttered, crossing her arms over her chest.

"Hey, I think you ought to add that to your menu at the inn." He winked. "Why, I bet they'd come beating down your front door from miles around!"

Though it was obvious he was jesting, Chyenna sputtered in reply. "No way! Not over my dead body!"

By now the girls were giggling so hard, Chyenna had no choice but to join in too, but not without first stealing another glance at Blair. His gaze locked with hers. Pushing back the rim of his Stetson, he winked again, his eyes laughing down at her. As the firelight played off his face, she couldn't help noting how he appeared so relaxed, so jovial—a rare event indeed. She wished she could catch the moment, hold on to it forever. Soon enough, they'd both be forced back to the real world, and the ever constant reminders of the barriers that separated them.

"Okay, everybody! Let's sing happy birthday," Blair announced. "But first, Lisa darlin', don't forget to make your wish."

"Not just one wish, Daddy. It's got to be three."

"All right then. Three."

Chyenna caught the look that passed fleetingly between Mandy and Lisa. Undoubtedly they were thinking back to the Star Party, that afternoon they'd first met and talked about wishes. *What Lisa's really wishing for is a family, a complete family. And as things stand with Blair, that would be a near impossibility . . .*

After Lisa had made her silent wishes and blown out the candles, they all dug in, smacking their lips and declaring the cake was the best they'd ever tasted.

"Seems like the llamas should be getting a piece of cake too," Lisa said between bites. "What I mean is, the idea for this campout all started when Dancer won her first blue ribbon."

"Cake wouldn't be good for them," Mandy answered in a pragmatic manner.

Nodding her agreement, Lisa glanced at the corral. "Oh, cool!" She bolted to her feet. Her eyes were wide, her voice filled with wonder. "Look, you guys!"

"Well, I'll be darned . . ." Blair's voice trailed as he stood up next to Lisa. Chyenna and Mandy promptly got to their feet also. In the soft purple dusk, the three llamas were prancing about in a wide circle, one directly behind the other. An orange harvest moon was peering over the east horizon and the first dazzling stars were poking through.

"They're pronking," Lisa said in a hush. "I can't believe it . . . this was one of my wishes . . . something

I've been wishing for a long time. This is why I named my llama Dancer . . ."

"What's pronking?" Mandy asked.

"I already told you last summer at the Star Party. It means dancing. And it doesn't happen very often." She lowered her voice again. "Just watch."

The llamas continued their stiff-legged gait. Then as if by magic, they propelled themselves through the air, all four feet leaving the ground and landing again in one swift, fluid motion.

"Wow," Chyenna breathed. "This is so beautiful. Unreal . . ."

"Unreal, for sure," Blair murmured, his gaze fixed on the llamas. She felt his arm go around her. "Lisa's right. This doesn't happen but once in a rare while."

Indeed the trusty llamas that had packed in their gear by day seemed transformed now. They appeared almost ghostly, mythical, as if in concert with some mysterious song heard only by them.

Lisa's voice was choked with emotion. "Thank you, llamas. Thank you for the best birthday present ever."

They remained there watching, not far from the campfire, all four arm-in-arm as the graceful creatures continued their dance.

The moon sailed higher and twilight melted into darkness. Then the dance ended, and all was right with the world.

* * *

Chyenna awoke and listened. The cabin was completely silent, save for the ticking of the clock on the shelf above her cot, plus the sound of the girls' even breathing from the bunk beds on the opposite side of the bedroom.

After dousing their campfire with plenty of water, they'd come back inside the cabin, popped some corn, drank apple juice, and played Monopoly until shortly after midnight.

To Chyenna it had all seemed so extraordinary, as if they *were* a real family; a reality some secret, ridiculous part of her was wishing for also. Then too, the afterglow of the llamas' dance had somehow lingered. Despite the gaiety, the talk and laughter, the good-natured banter that said, "Just as soon as I buy Park Place, I'm gonna wipe out your bankroll but good!"

Thirsty now, Chyenna sat up, dangling her feet over the side of the cot. Blair had opted to sleep on the daybed in the L-shaped living room that connected to the kitchen, while Chyenna and the girls occupied the one bedroom.

Padding her way toward the kitchen, she rubbed her eyes. She must have fallen to sleep the minute her head hit the pillow, she realized with fresh appreciation for the unpolluted air, sunshine, and physical exertion. My, what a glorious day it had been. Nighttime too.

Blair had left a small night-light plugged into the outlet next to the kitchen table. As she passed by it, she darted a look toward the daybed. She blinked, looking again. Blair wasn't there!

A pang of concern shot through her. Where was he? How long had he been gone? A quick survey of the cabin soon told her he was nowhere inside.

Maybe he's just stepped out for some more fresh air, she decided. Or to check on the llamas, although she couldn't imagine why that would be necessary. Oh yes! Now she knew. He was stargazing—or rather *observing*, as the astronomers called it. Still, he certainly hadn't packed in a telescope, not even binoculars as far as she knew . . .

She shrugged into her fleece-lined jacket, then hurried outside onto the covered front porch. Squinting, she peered past the sparse grove of trees that surrounded the cabin, beyond onto an open clearing. The full moon had bathed the landscape in its pearly glow, making it easy to detect his outline, Stetson and all, silhouetted against the lighted backdrop. He appeared to be sitting on a large rock or maybe it was a chair of some sort. At any rate, his back was turned to her.

Calling softly, she advanced in his direction. He stood up and whirled around.

"Looking at the stars?" she asked, keeping her voice light as she closed the distance between them.

"No. Except for what I can see with my bare eyes. It's next to impossible to do much serious observing during a full moon," he reminded her.

"Oh, of course." She tipped her head back and gazed heavenward at the star scattered sky. "But full moon or not, there's more to see here than was ever possible back in Portland. It's stunning . . ."

"L.A. too," he agreed.

"So if you're not observing, then what are you doing here?" She shivered. "It's predicted to hit freezing to-night. Matter of fact, I think it already has." With mock disapproval, she smiled up at him, all the while trying to keep her teeth from chattering. "You'll catch your death out here, Blair Westerman."

"And so could you, my little city gal." His answering smile was gentle, assessing. He stroked back her hair and tilted her chin up to his.

She couldn't resist him. "Hmm, but what a way to go," she murmured, melting into him. She felt his warm breath against her forehead, inhaled his clean masculine scent. "Oh, Blair. It feels so good here in your arms."

"You're just using that as an excuse to get warm," he teased. His fingers tunneled through her hair.

"You still haven't said *what* you're doing out here," she said.

"Just thinking. One has a tendency to do that on your kid's birthday, I suppose."

"And isn't it wonderful? Lisa getting her birthday wish, I mean . . . and all of us having the chance to see the llamas dance on the night of a harvest moon?"

"Uh-huh." He kissed the top of her head, held her a little tighter. "Know something, Chyenna?"

"What?"

"Your ex-husband was right. You *are* a romantic. It's just too bad he couldn't appreciate that in you. He was a fool, leaving you and Mandy like he did."

She pulled back a little, met his eyes. His gaze was intense, two deep dark pools. "If you ask me, you're quite the romantic yourself, Blair Westerman. It must be the poet in you . . ."

He chuckled. "You weren't supposed to find out about that, but give me three guesses and I'll only need one. Lisa told you, didn't she?"

"Uh-huh. And I happen to think that's marvelous."

"Hmm. Thanks."

"Blair?"

"Yes?"

"Dance with me. Please."

"What?" Subtle traces of confusion threaded his voice. "Here? Now?"

"Yes! We won't need music, the stars will sing for us. All we need to do is dance and listen . . ."

He pressed her to him, ran his hands up and down the length of her spine. Kissing her, he caught the scent of her lilac perfume, tasted her sweetness, felt her run-away heart.

Eagerly she lifted her mouth to receive his kiss as they swayed together in the moonlit meadow.

"Are the stars singing yet?" he rasped, cupping her face in his hands. "Can you hear them, my darling Chyenna?"

"Oh yes. Yes! They're singing . . . just for us." She shut her eyes as he drew her near again, holding her firmly but tenderly against him. His mouth slanted down on hers. Moments later—an eon perhaps—when she opened her eyes, she saw his were still tightly closed. Unspoken emotions strained his handsome features.

"Blair?"

"Hmm?" He opened his eyes, but his face remained unreadable.

"What's wrong?" The question vanished into nothingness.

An artery in his neck throbbed. "This isn't good . . . it's . . . it's all a big mistake. Sooner or later, we'll both regret it, Cheyenna."

She wanted to tell him how much she loved him, how he was everything she'd ever wanted, because she knew now with every shred of her being, it was true. But she couldn't. No, not now. He wasn't ready to hear it. He didn't *want* to hear it. He didn't want her love.

"Yes. Perhaps you're right. This . . . this is all wrong. Tomorrow morning we'll come to our senses and realize it even more." She tried to ease away, but his grasp wouldn't allow it. She heaved a sigh, succumbing once again to the wonder of his strong arms wrapped around her.

Slowly he traced a finger down her cheek, his gaze

soulful, haunted. Then he clasped her hand and pressed it to his mouth for a long, lingering moment.

"We'd better get back inside now." His voice was ragged, his face drawn. "You're right. Out here, we'll catch our death."

Chapter Eleven

Although it was nearly three in the morning, Blair couldn't sleep. Sitting up on the edge of his cot, he flicked on the old brass lamp next to him and blinked as his eyes adjusted to the sudden pool of bright light. His worn leather wallet was lying on the table next to the lamp where he'd tossed it earlier.

Reaching for the wallet, he flipped it open, then stared down at the two snapshots in the plastic insert. The first was of Martha. The second in the space facing it was Lisa's school picture, taken almost a year ago. He stared at both of them for an indefinite time. The resemblance was so uncanny, it made his throat tighten.

Martha. He narrowed his gaze on her smiling face and fought against that familiar old feeling. How many times since her death had he sat like this and stared at the photo? He bet a million, at least. But tonight the pain seemed somehow muted, more distant.

Unbidden, George's words echoed in his mind. It was almost as if they were still sitting together on the front porch steps that evening last summer. "Stop beating yourself up, brother . . . Martha was determined to get back to the city . . . there's nothing you could've done . . ." Maybe George was right. Maybe it was time for him to finally wake up and come to grips with that. Truth was, it didn't matter any longer *where* Martha had been living at the time of her death. She was gone. Gone forever and she'd never be coming back. No amount of self-blame could ever erase it.

Blair's mind skipped over to Lisa's birthday party, their evening campfire . . . the chocolate cake . . . and the glow on his daughter's face when they'd sung to her. This was Lisa's second birthday that had come and gone now since Martha had died. But tonight . . . well, things had been different. Yep, time was definitely marching on . . . and maybe that was good.

Then there was Chyenna, a real complication to be sure. How beautiful she'd looked with the moonlight reflecting against her hair. And their kisses had been out of this world. Bottom line was, she was scaring him half to death. She was causing him to take a long, cold hard look at himself—and he didn't like what he was seeing.

He got to his feet and started pacing. So what, really, was he seeing? A man numb with self-pity? A man stuck in the past? Yes, yes. Sadly, yes . . . but not any longer. From now on, things were gonna be different. He could feel it. Deep in his gut. Things would be different from now on because he *wanted* them to be. And his love for Chyenna was growing with each passing moment.

Heaving a sigh, he sat down again, then stared some more at Martha's glossy image. He felt his jaw working, but his eyes remained dry. Time, the healer of all wounds, they said. And he knew now that his healing had finally come. He was ready to make a lasting commitment—that is, if Chyenna would have him. One thing for certain, he intended on finding out tonight . . .

Hesitantly he touched his ex-wife's image with a trembling finger, and whispered, "I'll always remember you, babe. You'll always hold a special place in my heart. But it's time for me to move on now. It's time to start over."

Dawn crept over the land, bathing the hills, cliffs, and canyons with a silver-gray light. In the east, the sky was painted in splashes of rose-tinged lavender while the rising sun chased away a crisp autumn chill.

Chyenna awoke early, emerging from a restless sleep. After tiptoeing into the bathroom, she showered and washed her hair, then hurried into the kitchen to brew a pot of strong coffee. She suspected Blair needed that extra jolt of caffeine also. More than once she'd heard him stirring in the middle of the night, and guessed he hadn't slept any better than she had.

Luckily, the girls had seemed oblivious to all this, for the minute they'd said good night and turned out the lights, they'd fallen into exhausted, but contented slumbers. Luxuriating in the knowledge there'd be no early morning chores today, they'd probably sleep at least another couple of hours, Chyenna decided.

Measuring out the coffee, she took in the pungent fragrance of the freshly ground beans. Yes, she'd best make it strong for she was exhausted this morning. Exhausted and chagrined.

What had ever come over her last night? Why had she allowed herself to succumb to Blair's heart-stopping kisses, the fire in his eyes, his touch? Maybe it was because of the glittering stars or the splendid full moon . . . or perhaps even the llamas dancing their beguiling dance at twilight. Whatever, the spell had been cast . . . and she'd fallen prey.

Absently she listened to the water trickle through the coffee filter as she stared out the kitchen window. The sunlight was growing brighter, the frost in the meadow catching prisms of light. Perhaps she'd go for a short hike, try to clear her mind of its confusion, its muddied thoughts. Yes, she needed time to sort through it all, try to piece it together.

"Good morning." She gave a start.

"Good morning, Blair." She flashed him a bright smile, at the same time searching his face.

She saw nothing but a masked expression.

"Beautiful day," he said thickly.

"Yes, isn't it?" A disconcerting pause followed. She wrenched her gaze from his. "Coffee will be ready in a few minutes. Help yourself. I'll be gone for a while, not long. I'll have mine when I get back."

"Back?" He arched one eyebrow. "Back from where?"

"I . . . I was just planning on taking a hike . . . a short one . . . as I said, I won't be long."

"Like me to go with you?"

"No, not this time." She knotted her hand into a fist at her side. "I need to go alone."

"Oh. Whatever." He paused, then cleared his throat. "But may I at least make a recommendation? There're several trails bordering the property, but one in particular is better than the rest."

"Sure. Which one is it?" Again she gave him her brightest smile, though deep inside, her heart was beating harder than a trip hammer.

"Directly behind the corral, you'll see the trailhead with a signpost pointing northwest. It's a scenic hike from there up to Table Mountain, no more than a couple of miles and not too strenuous."

"Thanks. I'll check it out." She combed her fingers through her damp hair. "Isn't that the place where I heard you telling the girls you've camped out a time or two?

"Yep, and the view's spectacular." The first hint of a smile touched his lips. "Better go now. Be careful."

"I will. Thanks again." Brushing past him, steeling herself against the temptation to linger, she slipped into her navy blue windbreaker and hurried outside. The tension she'd just experienced, that ever raging turmoil had been almost insufferable. She was certain Blair had felt it too.

Yet as she started out, her spirits soon lifted. The morning sun was bright with promise, the air brisk and invigorating. Yes, she definitely needed this time alone here in this beautiful place. Goodness only knew, it might be quite a while until she had the opportunity to come here again—if, in fact, she ever did.

As she rounded the cabin, she breathed in the sweet scent of pine, heard the trill of birdsong. Dried leaves crunched beneath her feet. Overhead, an airplane droned. With the exception of Blair's and her unsettling tryst last night, the weekend at Mule Deer had been most extraordinary. This morning, she was certain, would be no exception.

Passing the corral, she noted that the llamas were once again grazing uneventfully as if last night's dance had been a mere dream. She blinked. Maybe it had. Maybe the whole crazy night had been nothing but a dream. Blair's kisses especially.

No, foolish woman, stop trying to kid yourself. His kisses were as real as real can be—and no amount of denial can ever change that.

But could their physical contact have indicated that Blair loved her too? No. She seriously doubted that.

At the trailhead, she began her ascent. Though the climb was gradual, she found herself breathing heavily, still one more reminder of the six-thousand-foot elevation. Yet where else would the air be so pristine, the wild flowers so profuse with bright colors, the silence so totally silent?

Sometime later, she paused to rest, bracing her hands on her hips and looking around. More orange and pink wildflowers grew from craggy outcroppings, though the scrub pine was becoming stunted, the soil rockier. A short distance away, two squirrels chased each other, kicking up tiny columns of dust, then disappeared behind a boulder.

Smiling, inhaling deeply again, she continued on. When she'd finally reached the top, she found a downed tree and paused to sit on a bare section of it. In the distance, stark rock formations were etched against the blue horizon while deeply carved canyons lay in shadows. A narrow green river twisted down an equally narrow gorge.

No wonder Blair liked to come here to do his night observing, she decided. It took little stretch of the imagination to realize how absolutely stunning the starry skies must be here. Then too, the horizons provided an astronomer's paradise, with very little obstructing the view on all sides.

For a fleeting instant, she wished she had allowed him to come with her now. Something as uplifting as this was meant to be shared. But no, she'd come here for solitude. The last thing she needed was Blair sitting here beside her, his powerful masculinity undermining her good intentions.

What happened last night had been nothing to Blair but lust, she reminded herself with a firm mental shake. And though she *did* love Blair, what good could come from it? He had undoubtedly let down is guard, then in the nick of time, put a slamming halt to what might have been. While they were locked in each other's arms, had he been imagining it was Martha instead? Perhaps she, Chyenna, had been a substitute for the woman he'd really wanted—until, of course, he'd come to his senses. The thought caused a shudder to ripple through her, make her stomach twist with mortification. How did she ever let herself to get in so deep?

But the truth was, it had happened, and there was no choice now but to take a chance, that leap of faith. She mustn't keep her love for him buried deep inside of her any longer. She must tell him. Very soon.

For loving Blair felt so right.

And at the same time, so wrong.

Yet if she didn't, if she failed to let him know, she was not only betraying herself, but a chance for their future together . . . if, in fact, that chance even existed. Truth was, she was not only a dreamer, but a risk-taker also. And this would most undoubtedly be the greatest risk of her life . . . even greater than her marriage to Daniel, her move to Prairie Valley, her struggle to make a go of her business.

For a long time she just sat there, her arms around her drawn-up knees, staring out at the rocky mesas in the distance, the deep yawning canyons, the endless sky.

Despite her every intention, self-doubt nagged at her. Did she have the nerve? Could she really go through with it? Could she put her heart on the line, chance his rejection, perhaps even his rebuke? What if he only laughed at her, twisting his mouth in scorn, reminding her he'd never bargained for a lasting relationship in the first place. The very thought left her heart in a quandary of mixed emotions: fear, hope, dread, longing, but mostly, humiliation. Yes, humiliation. What good would it be now to make Prairie Valley her home if Blair didn't love her too? If he told her she'd meant nothing more to him than a challenge, an amusing pastime?

Standing slowly, stretching, she glanced up at the sky. Dark clouds were rolling in from the south. How long had she been sitting here mulling things over? She'd better not linger any longer, chance getting caught in a sudden downpour or worse, an electrical storm. Besides, she'd told Blair she'd be gone only a short time.

She started back slowly, allowing her muscles to warm, her lungs to expand. Already she could feel a slight aching in her calves and maybe a minor case of shin splints. Today's hike, coupled with the three-hour pack trip yesterday, was beginning to take its toll. Right now the prospect of a long hot soak in her bathtub back home sounded mighty inviting.

Without warning she felt her footing give way, the ground crumbling beneath her. Falling, her head struck something sharp. The ground tilted crazily, but she just kept falling. Pain ripped through her. She thought she heard someone calling her name, but it sounded unreal, fantasy-like, so far far away . . .

Down, down, tumbling farther. *Jack fell down and broke his crown . . .* the singsong words danced inside her mind. Her head throbbed and she tasted the rank taste of blood.

And then mercifully . . . mercifully, darkness prevailed.

With difficulty, Chyenna forced her eyes open. Wavering images floated before her. She tried to swallow, but her throat felt parched and sore, as did her lips. Someone was holding her hand. She felt a tear trickle down one cheek, but wasn't sure if or why she was really crying.

"Chyenna . . . oh, thank God!"

She inhaled shakily. Her chest hurt. She looked left, then right, never once moving her head. Tubes. Tubes everywhere. "W-where am I?" She closed her eyes again, retreating back into that warm safe blanket of nothingness. On second thought, she didn't want to know. It was much better here, better than the world she just glimpsed a second ago . . .

"Chyenna. Wake up, please! Don't go back . . ."

"W-what?"

"Stay with us, darlin'. You're in the hospital . . . you took a bad fall. Keep your eyes open . . . please, Chyenna! Please!"

She did as the speaker asked . . . a familiar voice . . . so familiar. "Blair?" she murmured weakly, narrowing her focus on the man sitting alongside her. At last she saw him, his beautiful, wonderful profile. But there were dark circles under his eyes. And his brow was lined with deep wrinkles.

"Ma, go get the nurse," she heard him say over his shoulder. "Tell her to hurry."

"Blair," Chyenna repeated. This time it came as a confirmation, no longer a question. She offered him a trembling smile.

"Yes, Chyenna." He stroked her cheek, tucked back a strand of hair. "It's me." He gazed down at her at length before continuing. His expression was dark, his eyes troubled. "I was so worried . . . sick with worry."

"W-where . . . where am I?"

"Valley Memorial. You've been knocked out for over a day. Ma and Rusty came as soon as they got word. The girls are in good hands . . ."

"I fell," she said, trying to comprehend more fully. "I must've stepped too close to the edge . . . or maybe the ground was unstable. Anyway, all I remember was that I was falling and falling . . . and someone was calling my name." She shut her eyes briefly, then opened them again.

"That someone was me. I started getting worried

when the weather turned foul, so I came looking for you. Thank God I found you when I did. I should've remembered to warn you about the erosion up there on Table Mountain. The ground is very unstable near the ledge where you fell."

She touched her hand to her bruised face. "W-what happened to me? I mean, how did I end up here?"

"As I said, you got knocked out, plus you suffered three broken ribs and a number of bumps and bruises. You were airlifted off the mountain. Oh, Chyenna. You could've—" He broke off suddenly, releasing a shaky breath.

"Mandy . . . Lisa. Are . . . are they okay?"

"Yes. Quite worried, but fine."

She gave a small sigh of relief. "Good. Blair?"

"Hmm?"

"There . . . there's something I need to tell you . . ."

"Shh. Save your breath. We'll talk later . . ." He took her hand again in his and gave it a tender squeeze, but the gesture couldn't disguise the sudden warning note in his voice.

Chyenna was released from the hospital a short time later and in the days that followed, she recovered fully from her injuries—with the exception of an occasional headache and a sore back.

Her doctor had ordered that she rest at home for two full weeks, interspersed with a few sessions of physical therapy. Yet it wasn't until Nan had insisted the inn could carry on awhile longer without her—and Blair had readily agreed—that Chyenna was finally convinced to abide by those orders.

Meanwhile, life at the Triple Y Ranch ticked on in ordinary fashion. Blair and his brothers were busy weaning the calves and buttoning down the ranch in preparation for what had been predicted as an unusually harsh winter.

The girls, too, had returned to the normal routine of chores, school, and homework, in and around their ever constant giggles and chatter about their heartthrob, Billy Halligan. Though it had been nearly three weeks since Odyssey Productions had packed up their props and left, their pubescent ardor for him failed to dim. Life was anything but ordinary in Prairie Valley, though. Already renovations had started at the pool, with a new, more elaborate schedule of swimming and fitness classes in the works. Plans for the movie theater were in full swing also. Construction was slated to start sometime early the following spring.

Lisa was among the first to sing Chyenna's praises. "Now the kids won't have to drive into the hills to find something cool to do on Saturday nights or hang out on the corner across from the gas station."

"Yeah," Mandy had been quick to chime in, her chest puffed out with pride. "Everybody at school's saying my mom is the person who made this all happen."

It was common knowledge indeed now that these new improvements had been wrought, for the most part, by Chyenna. If it hadn't been for the public stir she'd caused when she'd renovated the inn, people were saying, Odyssey Productions would've likely never visited Prairie Valley in the first place.

Yet while Chyenna was grateful for this new show of acceptance, what really mattered most now was Blair Westerman. One afternoon after he had made what was now becoming his daily, obligatory visit, Chyenna decided it was now or never. If she had to wait a millisecond longer to tell him how much she loved him, she was certain she would simply turn up her toes and die.

Granted, these past two weeks, Blair had seemed to retreat into his typical taciturn world. But whether he was ready now to accept her love for him, she could no longer wait to find out. Goodness only knew, because of the accident, she'd already been detained far longer than she'd wanted. No, she simply couldn't allow this seemingly insurmountable wall to stand in her way anymore.

She was sitting at her desk in the family quarters when she heard Blair's familiar rap on her door. She got up to answer it.

"Mornin'." He touched the brim of his Stetson, his mouth quirked in a cautious half-smile.

"Good morning, Blair. Come in."

"What's this?" he asked, glancing down at the catalogue of culinary supplies she was holding in her hand. "You're supposed to be resting, not working," he added with mock disapproval.

"I *am* resting." She smiled up at him, but her insides

were quaking. "Nothing that taxing about placing a few orders, is there?"

"Nope. Suppose not."

As he followed her into the front room, she gestured to an empty chair. "Have a seat. Care for a cup of coffee?" *Stop stalling. Get to the point. This conversation is sounding absolutely inane.*

"Thanks, but I can't," he replied. "I'm short on time. I had to stop at the tack shop on the way home from dropping the girls off at school."

He looked so wonderful, wearing a camel-colored fleece shirt that accentuated last summer's tan and worn, tight-fitting jeans. It was taking every shred of willpower to keep from throwing herself into his arms, telling him it didn't matter how much he still loved Martha, that her love for him knew no bounds. Yet she couldn't avoid the reality of his rigid stance, the cautiousness in his voice, the way he was looking at her.

"Blair." She swallowed against the knot in her throat. "There's something we need to talk about. Now. Please don't rush off. And don't put me off."

"Yeah, you're right." He lowered himself onto the chair and removed his hat, toying with it.

As she sat down across from him, her heart raced with anticipation. "That day in the hospital . . . when I woke up . . . I wanted to tell you I'd fallen in love with you. You were the first one I saw looking down at me . . . and it was the first thing that popped into my mind . . ."

"I had something to tell you too," he interrupted. "But . . . but I thought it better . . . better to wait." His face was rigid with pent-up emotion, which only served to escalate her own wariness.

"Wait? What do you mean, wait?"

"It . . . it just didn't seem right then . . . you just coming out of the concussion and all . . ."

In the space of a heartbeat, the words she must've silently rehearsed a thousand times or more vanished. Her stomach clenched as she waited for him to continue.

"A couple of weeks ago, after our night at Mule Deer, I made a promise to myself." Setting his Stetson on the floor, he linked his hands tightly beneath his knees and studied them. "I knew I'd fallen in love with you, Chyenna. I was ready to start over . . ." His voice turned ragged. "But . . . but then came the accident . . . and everything suddenly changed."

"You love me too?" she asked in a small voice.

"Yes. But not in the way you *need* to be loved." The silence that followed could have lasted a millennium. "What . . . what I'm trying to say is, after I found you hurt so bad . . . I . . . I knew I just couldn't go through it again. It was too much like the time before . . . with Martha." He squared his jaw, then righted it again. "I didn't want that to happen, Chyenna. God only knows I didn't . . ."

"I can wait it out, Blair," she murmured. "I can wait for however long it takes."

"No." He met her gaze. Anguished blue eyes locked

with hers. "It won't work. I . . . I can't risk losing you too."

She blinked rapidly, struggling to keep her tears at bay. "But I'm fine now, Blair. The doctor's practically given me a clean bill of health."

"Yes, thank God. But there's no guarantee something couldn't happen again . . . to any of us." His voice broke. "We . . . we must let go of each other. For good."

She stood up slowly. Her feet felt like lead. Her heart like cold hard stone. "Shall I leave, Blair? Move away from here?"

"No. That's not what I meant. That wouldn't be fair to you."

Disbelief and anger washed over her as she struggled to make some sense of it all. She turned her back to him, lest he see the tears she could no longer hold back. "But how can we go on pretending we're nothing but neighbors after all we've been through?"

"I don't know. We'll find a way." His voice sounded flat, wooden as he added, "I'm sorry, darlin'. I truly am."

Hugging her chest with her arms, she remained as motionless as a statue, head lowered, back still turned.

At last she heard the door close behind him and the clap of his footsteps as he retreated down the stairs.

Shoulders hunched, Blair trudged doggedly back to his pickup. What had he just done? Why had he just told the woman he wanted for the rest of his life they must go their separate ways? Did he know how much he was losing? Would he, sometime in the future, look back on this day and kick himself in the rear? Of course he would. The answer was so painfully brutal.

Pausing, he inhaled sharply the frigid air, tipped his head back and gazed up at the stars. There they were, always, those countless tiny suns that stretched far beyond all imagining, touching the very edge of the vast, dark universe. Yep, he couldn't deny it, Chyenna was *his* shining star, a light that had intruded into his world of darkness.

But now that light would journey on, to distant worlds, to someone else's arms. How could he have been such a fool to turn her away?

Chapter Twelve

"**S**hould I put the box of china with the dining room or the kitchen stuff, ma'am?"

"The dining room, please." Chyenna looked up from her packing and flashed a polite smile at the portly moving-van driver.

Now one week later, on an overcast Saturday afternoon, a van marked *Continental Movers and Storage* sat in the empty parking lot of the Stagecoach Inn.

Chyenna and Blair were indeed through. The only way she could escape the pain, Chyenna was certain, was by foregoing her option to buy the inn and leaving Prairie Valley. She and Mandy would soon be on their way to Portland, back to the condo she'd secured a few days earlier.

While the movers loaded boxes, crates, and furniture, Chyenna ticked off reminders to herself on her to-do list. All week long, matter of fact, she'd immersed herself in a whirlwind of activity: last-minute packing, cleaning, delivering staples from the restaurant to charity, and finally, earlier that day, turning in her keys to the landlord. Yet for all her busyness, she functioned as if in a trance. And if anyone were to look cross-eyed at her, she couldn't trust herself not to collapse into a torrent of tears.

Mandy, also, wasn't holding up too well. When Chyenna had informed her about the sudden turn of events, her daughter had banished herself to her room, sobbing hysterically.

Thank goodness Mandy was with her 4-H club right now, Chyenna thought as she affixed strapping tape to the last box of linens. Just seeing the movers hard at work would've no doubt sent Mandy into further despondency. The club leader had taken the kids to the mall in Blakeston to participate in a youth development display.

Chyenna checked her watch: two forty-five. Blakeston was about an hour away and the girls were due back at three. That meant she and Mandy could most likely be on the road and over the Mount Hood Pass before total darkness set in. Chyenna planned to leave shortly ahead of the van so she could have the condo unlocked and ready. Though weather reports forecasted snow flurries later that night, if all went as planned, they should be able to beat the storm.

Restless, she wandered over to the window and stared out over the backyard. The river had risen considerably since summertime, and was running swiftly now, cascading over rocks and rotting tree limbs. Though the banks were still edged in yellow, orange and burnt umber, many of the deciduous trees were beginning to shed their leaves. The hills were shrouded in gray mist, and a watery sun was poking through patches of clouds. She sighed. So beautiful. So achingly magnificent . . .

Yet the truth nagged at her like a festering sore. All the loveliness, the life affirming essence, only paled in comparison to losing Blair. How could she turn her back and walk away? How could life ever have meaning again without him?

She turned and watched the two men hard at work as they hauled Mandy's four-poster bed out through the front door. Meanwhile, she'd shut Mandy's cat in the empty spare bedroom with food, fresh water, and a litter box. From the first moment the moving van had arrived, the feline had appeared to sense something was going on. To Mandy, it would be the very last straw if the cat escaped and ran away, Chyenna realized. Her daughter was already losing far too much . . .

The phone rang. She hurried to answer it. "Yes? Yes, this is Chyenna. Of course, Jenny, I know you're the 4-H leader. What is it?"

Fear lay over her as she heard Jenny's panicked reply. "Oh, Chyenna, I hate to tell you this, but we've got a problem! We're still in the mall, at the main entrance. . . . Lisa and Mandy were supposed to meet us here over an hour ago!"

"What? You mean they didn't?"

"That's right! We've looked high and low . . . I just can't imagine what—Oh Chyenna, wait! Hold on! Mall security is here . . . they need to talk . . ."

The wait seemed like an eternity. *Oh, please God! Please let this be nothing but a big misunderstanding!* Chyenna's heart thudded, her palms grew cold and clammy. She could hear Jenny speaking in muffled tones, her hand cupped over the receiver.

At last she was back. "Chyenna! You still there?"

"Yes! Of course! What did they say?"

"Nothing but routine questions . . . asked what the girls were wearing, that sort of thing."

Sudden panic gripped Chyenna. "Well, aren't they going to *do* something? I mean—"

"I'm gonna have to cut this short," Jenny interrupted. "Looks like security still has more questions. And oh, one more thing . . . I've been calling Lisa's father, too, but his line's busy. Would you try to get through to him, please? It looks as if I might be tied up here for a while yet."

"Certainly!" Chyenna shoved all personal matters aside. "I'll get right on it."

Her hands were shaking so badly, she could barely set the phone back in the cradle. Her mind went blank. Oh dear, what was Blair's number anyway?

At last it came to her and she managed to dial. Busy! She hung up, then wrung her hands as she waited. A minute later, she tried again. Her stomach sank. Still busy. Releasing a sigh, she snatched her jacket off the coat tree, grabbed her car keys and purse, and dashed down the stairs, only to run headlong into Blair at the bottom.

"Oh!" she exclaimed, nearly dropping her purse. Her forehead throbbed where she'd collided with his hard, solid chest.

"There's news! Bad news!" she blurted.

"I know! I already heard." His eyes were wild with desperation, his jaw set tight. "Grab your toothbrush and maybe a change of clothes. We gotta go! *Right* now!"

"But the van is due to leave! Mandy and I are supposed to leave soon!"

He lowered his voice, leveling her with a "get real" look. "Wake up, Chyenna. Mandy isn't here. You're not going anywhere now except with me."

"Oh, Blair." She choked back a sob as the truth set in. "What're we going to do?" She longed to nestle herself into the shelter of his embrace. Feel his warm, strong arms wrapped around her once again. But she couldn't, wouldn't.

And he didn't give any indication he wanted her to.

"What are we going to do?" he echoed brusquely. "We're gonna go after them, that's what! Hurry! I'll explain the rest after we get started . . ."

*   *   *

"So what is it?" Chyenna asked as they sped south down the two-lane asphalt highway. The road twisted and turned through a narrow canyon. Dark shadows loomed up on both sides.

He kept his eyes fixed straight ahead, avoiding her gaze. "Just before I came for you, I got a call from one of Lisa's friends who, unfortunately for us, wasn't willing to give me her name." He gripped the steering wheel tighter. "The girl said Lisa had asked her to phone me *after* she and Mandy had had enough time to get out of town."

"*What?* They ran away?" Chyenna's head reeled. She pressed her fisted hand to her lips in an attempt to stifle her rising fright.

"Yeah." He gave a humorless laugh. "But they didn't want us to worry. Can you believe that?"

"Did . . . did this girl tell you where they were going?"

"Yep, she sure did." He scowled. "Our daughters left from the Greyhound bus station in Blakeston. They're headed for L.A.—Universal Studios. They planned their getaway last night on the phone."

"L.A.!" She inhaled shakily, scarcely believing her ears. "And you're intending to drive all the way to southern California?" The rolling buttes, huge dark mounds against the purple-gray horizon, seemed to pass by in slow motion.

"I'll do whatever it takes," he snapped. "All this because of good ole' Billy Halligan. According to our anonymous informant, our daughters were bound and determined to see him again. At least Lisa's friend was willing to take down my number—" he gestured toward his cell phone lying on the console between them, "—in case the girls contact her with another message for us."

Chyenna closed her eyes and rested her head against the back of her bucket seat. No. This couldn't be happening. Not Mandy. Not Lisa.

After opening her eyes, she glanced at the clock on the dashboard. It was already close to three-thirty. The more she heard of Blair's explanation, the more she realized her chances of leaving town any time soon were growing slimmer by the minute. Then too, she'd rushed off in such a hurry, she'd completely forgotten to communicate with the moving-van driver.

Reaching inside her purse and extracting her own cell phone, she called the pager number engraved on the Continental Movers business card. In a matter of minutes, her answer came.

"Hello? Mr. Karson? Ralph Karson? Uh . . . yes, this is Chyenna Dupres. I'm the one who left in the pickup a little while ago," she added unnecessarily.

"Yeah, yeah." The man's voice was filled with exasperation. "More like took off like a bat outta hell, you did. You headed back now, ma'am? Me and my buddy here, we got all your stuffed packed. We're due in Portland some time tonight, you know."

"Yes, yes, I *do* know that. But I'm afraid there's going to be a delay." She paused, cupping her hand over the phone. "They want to go *now*," she hissed to Blair.

"Tell 'em to can it. This is an emergency, for God's sake."

Ignoring Blair's abrupt suggestion, she explained haltingly about the girls' disappearance. "I'm so sorry about all this, Mr. Karson . . . I really am."

"Ah, don't sweat it, ma'am." His voice softened. "I'm sorry I came on to you so abrupt like. I've got a daughter too."

"Look, I have a suggestion." She waved one hand in the air as she talked. "When you're ready to leave, just lock up and book yourself for a night at the Hitching Post Motel, three blocks east of Main. Add it to my bill, of course."

"Thanks, but my buddy and me . . . well, we'd rather hold out a little longer in the hopes we can still split. There's a huge snowstorm on the way—the worst blizzard in years, they say. We'd like to hit the road before it comes. You folks should be careful too."

"Yes, I heard the report." She glanced over at Blair, who by now was driving at least ten miles over the speed limit. "But my . . . er . . . my friend here—the other girl's father—I'm sure he intends to keep going regardless of the weather."

"Okie dokie. Suit yourself. Buzz me again in about an hour. Maybe by then you'll have found your kids. Good luck, ma'am. Good luck to both of you."

"Thanks. I'll stay in touch."

Blair snapped on the radio. "Don't waste your breath repeating what he said about the weather. I've already heard. Let's see now if we can get an update."

"Heavy snow is predicted in the entire Cascade mountain range for later tonight and most of tomorrow," the announcer was saying. "Winds are expected at around sixty miles per hour, giving way to white-out conditions. Traction devices are required on all Oregon mountain passes."

Fighting off a new wave of panic, Chyenna stared unseeingly out her side window. The sky was cobalt gray. So far, only a light drizzle prevailed. She hoped against all hope the weather reports would prove wrong.

Silently they kept driving. The sun was about to set, casting a rosy patch through the break in the clouds. Power lines stretched across the horizon like a giant erector set. They passed by a dilapidated barn, a deserted truck-stop cafe with one solitary gas pump outside. A minute later, they turned onto the four-lane highway and continued south.

"Shouldn't we be notifying the state patrol?" she asked. As if a silent covenant had been established between them, they continued to avoid each other's eyes.

"I already did. I also filled out a missing persons report. The cops checked out the Greyhound station, said that two girls who fit our daughters' description left on the one-thirty bus. Good thing it isn't an express."

"Why?"

"Because that'll give us the chance to try to head them off, hopefully at Kaiser," he replied as he rounded the next bend. The highway started to climb. Groves of pine edged each side of the road. "The cops also said they'd enter the girls' names in the NCIC—the National Crime Information Center—plus notified the LAPD."

Chyenna shuddered. Already she could visualize the girls' photos on one-gallon milk cartons, plastered on storefront windows. Her little girl, her baby! How could this be happening?

"As I see it," Blair went on, "this entire ordeal is a two-edged sword. We can breathe a little easier knowing that the girls weren't abducted, but by the same token, their case probably won't get top priority."

"Correction." She shifted uneasily. "They weren't abducted when they first left. But that doesn't mean something terrible still couldn't happen." Chyenna's thoughts tumbled inside her head. Had their impending move somehow prompted this? If she had decided to do the impossible and stay in Prairie Valley, would Lisa and Mandy have even conjured up such an outlandish idea? And exactly *whose* idea had it been in the first place?

But it was too late now to place blame. Too late and too irrelevant. Those moot issues didn't matter anymore. They'd already been through all that. The reality was, she and Blair were through. All that mattered now was making sure the girls got home safely.

"Damn." He slammed a fist against the steering wheel

and muttered something she couldn't hear. "Why, of all the godforsaken places, did Lisa have to get such a hair-brained notion to run back to L.A.? *Why?* After all I've gone through to get her out of there!"

She shook her head. Other than the obvious—Lisa's preteen attraction to Billy Halligan—she, too, was at a loss for answers. What a cruel turn of events. What a paradox for Blair.

"I hope you realize this is really very uncomfortable for me," she said, her thoughts turning back to her own well-being. "I mean, I didn't plan on seeing you again. I already figured we'd said our good-byes."

"My sentiments exactly," he answered tersely. "I guess we have our daughters to thank for this."

"Yes, we certainly do."

"I never told you to move away, you know."

She lifted one shoulder. "You might as well have. After all, what else can I do?"

You can stay right here, my darling! Give me one more chance! I love you, Chyenna. More than you'll ever know.

He didn't answer.

They drove on in silence, the tension so brittle, Chyenna was certain now she was about to snap. Already, even before she'd left town, she'd missed him miserably. She would keep on loving him forever, no matter how he insisted his love for her was insufficient. But if she told him that, he'd only laugh at her, tell her she was nothing but a foolish dreamer. Just as Daniel had.

Blair's words pierced through her thoughts. "I think you'd better call the pager again. Tell the movers they should go on without you."

Chyenna did as he said. This time, the call-back came through immediately. "Yes, sir," she said, nodding. "I understand. Just store my things in your warehouse after you get to Portland. And oh, by the way, would you please take my cat next door? To the Triple Y Ranch? I'm sure the folks there won't mind. Besides, they already understand the circumstances."

Angling Blair a cautious look, she set the phone back down. His expression was closed. More silence reigned. It was starting to snow now, large dry flakes, which swirled across the highway. The windshield wipers groaned beneath the snow's weight.

Her eyes were growing heavy and she stifled a yawn. How she could even think of dozing at a time like this, she wasn't sure. She was simply too numb, too exhausted to try to figure it out.

She stole a quick look at Blair. His handsome, rugged profile was etched against the purple twilight; his lips compressed in a tight line, his narrowed eyes intent. How many times she had immersed herself in those blue depths, allowed his beautiful lips to work their magic? She longed to reach out to him, assure him everything would turn out all right. But empty assur-

ances were worthless, a sham. Just like her love for him
that had remained so one-sided.

Please Blair, she silently pleaded before slipping off
to sleep. Please help me forget I ever loved you . . .

Blair massaged the tension at back of his neck as he
kept driving. He thought about Ma and Rusty, felt a trifle guilty that he hadn't called them yet. It'd be a smart
thing to do, but . . . but no, he would wait a little while
longer, till it was absolutely necessary. No point worry-
ing them yet. How he dreaded telling them that Lisa
was missing, had run off to Hollywood after some fool
movie star who still wasn't even dry behind the ears.

The snow slanted against the windshield in driving
white sheets. Blair shifted into four-wheel drive and ex-
pertly manuevered the truck around the next curve. He
darted a sideways glance at Chyenna. She appeared to
be sleeping, head tilted to one side, lips slightly parted.
Yes, those full, lush lips, just begging to be kissed. She
looked more beautiful than ever, her dark eyelashes
fanning her porcelain face, her auburn hair tousled,
falling in strands around her shoulders.

Something inside of him yearned to memorize every
angle and plane, every lovely inch of her. Yes, in only a
matter of time now, all he'd have left were the memories. Their kisses in the hayloft . . . dancing cheek-to-
cheek under the stars . . . that morning at the upper
ranch when he'd gone looking for her, eager to tell her
how much he loved her. Yet when he'd found Chyenna

lying bruised and unconscious, his entire world caved in. Again. Yep, fate had done a number on him all right, given him a stinging reminder of what more loss might cost him.

He shook his head. Man, how he loved her. And his love, he knew, was much, much more than just physical, a way to fill his lonely hours. His love had transcended far beyond that, something too fragile and beautiful to let go.

Pulling his lower lip through his teeth, he mulled over his place in the giant scheme of things. Though he'd stayed away from church this past year or so, he still considered himself a God-fearing man. And while he didn't believe that the Almighty had allowed the girls' disappearance as a punishment, he nevertheless found himself praying. *Please God. Please let Lisa and Mandy be safe. And . . . and if you could just send them home, I'll make you a deal. I'll take you up on what you've been trying so hard to give me. Chyenna. My future wife. My destiny, my everything. But there's something you're gonna have to realize, God. You can only give, and I can only take. The rest, of course, is up to Chyenna . . .*

Chyenna slowly opened her eyes, then blinked in confusion. Where was she? Why wasn't she home? Oh, yes . . . now she remembered. She was here with Blair in his pickup, driving into this dark, stormy night. She must've dozed off, but for how long she wasn't sure.

Mandy! Mandy, where are you? Oh dear God, please keep her safe. Watch over Mandy and Lisa both. Send them back home.

Chyenna stretched out her arms and yawned.

"Feel better?" Blair asked.

"A little . . . as good as I can under the circumstances." She blinked again. "How far have we come?"

"We're almost at the exit to Indianhead Springs. After that, in another twenty miles or so, we'll be coming to Kaiser."

She nodded. Without warning she spied the outline of a large vehicle ahead, much larger than a car or mid-sized RV. Its bright red taillights were barely visible through the driving snow.

"Look!" she exclaimed, pointing. "Maybe that's the Greyhound! Maybe that's the bus the girls are on!" She sat up straighter, fully awake now, her nerves once again on edge. "See if you can catch up. But be careful!"

Blair didn't need to be asked twice. In the space of a heartbeat, he'd floored the gas pedal and switched to the fast lane, cruising down the highway until they were alongside the bus, neck and neck. Yes, it was definitely a bus all right. But the logo on the side read *Ramose West Coast Tours.*

Fresh disappointment washed over Chyenna. She inhaled shakily to keep from bursting into tears. Blair only shook his head in frustration.

The snow was mixed with hail now. It drummed against the truck roof. The swish of a car in the next lane grew stronger, then dimmed. Headlights from the oncoming vehicles cut swathes through the darkness.

"I'm gonna take that next exit," Blair announced. "I think there's a small all-night hamburger joint not far down the road. Right now a strong cup of coffee sounds mighty—" The ringing of the cell phone cut him off midsentence. He glanced down at Chyenna's phone, then realized the sound was coming from his own.

"Yes?" He barked. "Oh, Ma! Hi! Yes, yes."

Chyenna strained to hear, but Sharon's voice was too faint. "They *what?* Are you sure?" The tiny lines at the corners of his eyes creased. He broke into a weary smile, shaking his head.

"Please, Blair. What is it?" Chyenna interrupted, unable to contain herself any longer.

"Hold on, Ma. I've got to tell Chyenna." White teeth flashed in a tight smile. "The girls had second thoughts . . . realized it was foolish to try to go so far, so when the bus stopped in Kaiser, they told the driver they weren't going any farther. They got off and called Rusty to come and get them. They're with Ma and Rusty right now," he said heaving a sigh, "playing Monopoly and eating popcorn, of all things!"

Chyenna sagged with relief. "Oh, thank God! Thank God," she said over and over.

"Ma? You still there? Listen. We're about twenty minutes or so from your place—well, actually in this weather, make it more like an hour. Tell the girls we'll be there soon. What? You think we should all stay for the night? Well . . . yeah, I guess that's not such a bad idea."

"Blair." Chyenna tugged on the sleeve of his jacket. "Let me talk to Mandy. Please."

"Hold on a minute, Ma. Put Mandy on." He switched the phone over to Chyenna.

"Mandy . . . are . . . are you all right?" she asked through gritted teeth.

"Yes, Mama. I'm doing great." The line went quiet. "I . . . I'm sorry, Mama. I didn't want to make you worry."

"Didn't want to make us worry?" Chyenna's voice raised. "We've been worried sick, Mandy! I don't know what Blair intends to do with Lisa, but as far as you go, young lady, you're grounded!"

"Mama, please. Just let me explain. It's . . . it's just that me and Lisa . . . well, it's like . . . like we knew we'd never see each other again. And we wanted to see Billy too . . . but that was stupid . . . we know that now. And . . . and well, anyway, we're having lots of fun right now with Lisa's grandma and Rusty. Besides, Billy was kind of stuck on himself. It would've been a big hassle going to see him."

"Well, I'm certainly glad to hear you figured that out in the nick of time."

"Oh, right, but there's something else. Something really, really important. Lisa's here too. She wants to talk to her dad. She'll tell him what it is . . ."

Shaking her head, Chyenna handed the phone back to Blair. "Your turn again."

"Lisa?" His voice was husky with checked emotion. "You're darned right I'm angry, but we'll settle that later." His voice broke. "I love you, sweetheart."

Chyenna watched the play of emotions parade across his face. Relief. Anger. But most of all, love.

Blair took the next exit, but instead of stopping for coffee, he just kept driving.

"Where are we going?" Chyenna asked.

"To Indian Trail Springs."

They meandered their way through sparse forests of pine until they came to the broad, flat mountaintop. Blair parked the truck and cut the motor. Stars peeked out through the rapidly parting clouds. Moonlight reflected off the virgin snow like a million crystals.

"Oh, how beautiful," Chyenna breathed. "It's . . . it's almost like a fairyland . . . and so quiet. So utterly quiet here."

"I thought you'd like it." He pulled her closer, enveloping her in the crook of his arm. "Some consider the sky even more outstanding this time of year than the sky in summer." He pointed up to Orion, the huge constellation to the south. The Mighty Hunter's three-starred belt winked back down at them.

She smiled, looking around. "I do think we're parked in the spot where Mandy and I pitched our tent."

He shook his head. "Wrong. This was the place where I'd parked my van. This is where you climbed inside and I missed out seeing you stark naked."

"Blair!" She laughed again. "You *would* remember a thing like that."

Blair's grip tightened. He turned, searched her face.

Lisa said something to me tonight," he started raggedly, "something so touching I didn't know whether to laugh or cry."

"Oh? What?"

"She said there was more than one reason she and your daughter decided to run away—and they hoped like crazy it would pay off in the end."

He traced the outline of her lips, caressed her cheek with his thumb. Their eyes caught again. A warm feeling spiraled inside of her. "What . . . what are you talking about?"

"Lisa told me that besides wanting to see Halligan again, she and Mandy were also scheming up a reason to get us back together." One corner of his mouth quirked into a half smile. "So they ran away. They knew we'd have to get together long enough until they were found, and they hoped that while we were at it, we'd rethink a few things."

She gave a nervous little laugh. "Kids!"

He nodded, then sent her an answering smile. "That morning at the upper ranch after you'd left for your hike, I decided to write a verse or two about how much I loved you. I . . . I was gonna give it to you . . . after you came back, of course . . . but then you took that tumble . . . and everything suddenly changed." He dipped his head shyly. "Will you give me another chance, Chyenna? Would you allow me to read it aloud to you now?"

"Oh, Blair. Yes . . . of course." Her words came in barely a whisper.

He dug into his jacket pocket, pulled out his wallet, and unfolded a frayed square of paper. Then he switched on the overhead light and cleared his throat.

"Here goes," he said, inhaling deeply. "For Chyenna."

"If stars were wishes, I'd reach for the sky,
I would clasp the brightest, no matter how high,
I'd make you a crown so sparkling and bright,
Then kiss your sweet lips all through the night.

And when the daylight put out the stars.
I would catch you a sunbeam, no matter how far,
I'd make you a necklace so brilliant with love,
The angels would sing from Heaven above.

"Alas, my darlin', I'm an ordinary man.
The stars and the sunbeams only slip through my hand.
All I can offer from the depths of my soul
Is a love to last forever and a heart that's full.

"So please say you love me, give me one more chance,
And we'll dance forever, a glorious dance,
For Chyenna, my darling, I want you as my wife.
To have, to hold, to cherish for the rest of my life."

When he'd finished reading, he pulled her closer and kissed the tip of her nose. "Well?" he asked softly.

Tears of happiness welled up in her eyes, spilled down her cheeks. Through her watery view of the world, she could only murmur wonderingly. "Oh, Blair. That's . . . that's the most wonderful, most beautiful poem I've ever heard." They came together in a long, sweet kiss.

"Is that supposed to mean it's a go?" he asked after they'd broken the contact. He framed his large hands on each side of her face, his eyes sparkling with anticipation.

"Oh yes, Blair! Yes, yes, yes!"

There on that snowy mountaintop, they kissed again and sealed their future forevermore.